GNoME
is
where
your
Heart
is

GNOME

is where your

Heart

is

GREENWILLOW BOOKS

AN IMPRINT OF HARPERCOLLINS PUBLISHERS

Gnome Is Where Your Heart Is
Text copyright © 2023 by Casey Lyall
Illustrations copyright © 2023 by Andy Smith

www.harpercollinschildrens.com
The text of this book is set in Tiempos Text.
Book design by Sylvie Le Floc'h

Library of Congress Cataloging-in-Publication Data
Names: Lyall, Casey, author.
Title: Gnome is where your heart is / by Casey Lyall.
Description: First edition. | New York : Greenwillow Books, an Imprint of HarperCollins Publishers, 2023. | Audience: Ages 8-12. | Audience: Grades 4-6. | Summary: Eleven-year-old Lemon Peabody is certain that aliens visited her grandfather thirty years ago, but she is running out of time to prove it before Grandpa Walt's memory fades.
Identifiers: LCCN 2022049163 (print) | LCCN 2022049164 (ebook) | ISBN 9780063239821 (hardcover) | ISBN 9780063239845 (ebook)
Subjects: CYAC: Extraterrestrial beings—Fiction. | Grandfathers—Fiction. | Alzheimer's disease—Fiction. | Best friends—Fiction. | Friendship—Fiction. | Humorous stories. | Science fiction. | LCGFT: Humorous fiction. | Science fiction. | Novels.
Classification: LCC PZ7.1.L94 Gn 2023 (print) | LCC PZ7.1.L94 (ebook) | DDC [Fic]—dc23
LC record available at https://lccn.loc.gov/2022049163
LC ebook record available at https://lccn.loc.gov/2022049164
23 24 25 26 27 LBC 5 4 3 2 1
First Edition

Greenwillow Books

For my grandparents:
Elaine, Tony, Patt, Gus, and Ferg

GNoME
is
where
your
Heart
is

CHAPTER 1

The golden rule of Shady Elms Retirement Home was listed clearly on the front door:

No unaccompanied minors on the premises after six p.m.

Which was why I was not using the front door.

"Dumb rule doesn't even make sense," I grumbled as I pulled myself up on Grandpa Walt's window ledge. As soon as I got into the room, I wouldn't *be* unaccompanied.

So there.

I dug the toes of my shoes into the brick wall and braced my elbows on the sill. "Grandpa!" I called through the screen. "Grandpa?" Silence, and then—

"NnnNNNaaaAaaaaghghgHhhh."

Squishing my face against the screen, I squinted into the

dim room. Grandpa Walt was sprawled out in his easy chair, asleep, glasses half off his face. He snuffled before releasing another monster snore.

Right. I forgot about the post-dinner nap. Trying to wake Grandpa usually took more noise than I was willing to risk, so I tested the window screen. Nope. He forgot to leave it unlocked.

"Grandpa?" I tried again.

"*NNNnnnAAAaghghGHh.*"

Definitely on my own here.

Balancing my weight on the windowsill, I pushed on the screen. It wiggled a bit. Switching my angle, I piled on the pressure when I felt it start to give. Hah hah! Victory!

The screen flew onto the floor of Grandpa's room with a clatter and I fell headlong over the sill, stomach pressed up against the frame as my legs dangled outside.

I was mostly inside, though, so still a win.

Grandpa Walt jerked awake with a snort, blinking bleary blue eyes around the room. "Wha—?"

"Heeeey, Grandpa," I said, giving him an upside-down wave. "Help, please?"

He stared at me, and worry began to itch at the back of my mind.

"Hello, dear," he said finally, straightening his glasses with a smile. "Did I know you were coming over?"

"We talked about it yesterday, remember?"

"Of course, of course." He shook his head and peered at the floor. "Is that my screen?"

Relief swamped through me as I flapped a hand at the broken window. "I will definitely fix that." Pop the square thing back in the square thing. How hard could it be?

"Hmm, my toolbox is around here somewhere." He scratched at his chin. My legs were starting to go numb as the window ledge cut off my circulation.

"*GRANDPA.*"

"Ooooh, one sec." Grandpa Walt pushed himself up out of his chair, wincing as his knees cracked. He grabbed his cane and started a slow shuffle over to the window. "Be right there, sweet pea. Hang on." He grinned. "This is quite the pickle you've gotten yourself into."

I kicked my feet in the air with a grunt. "Can we save the jokes for when I'm right-side up?"

Cackling, Grandpa Walt grabbed the waistband of my pants and yanked me forward. I popped through the gap and tumbled onto the floor with a crash. I lay spread-eagled on the rug, catching my breath. A few clonks and bruises, but I'd live.

The rubbery tip of a cane poked at my nose. "And why couldn't you use the front door?"

"Nurse Edie was on the desk." You'd think the overlord

of Shady Elms would take Saturday off, but apparently not. I dusted off my knees and stood up . . . only to pause at the look on Grandpa's face. The one he gets when he's trying to figure out the pieces he's forgotten and doesn't want me to know.

"If anyone's going to enforce the 'no kids visiting alone after six p.m.' rule, it's the big boss lady, right?" I prompted him with a little smile.

"Right," he said slowly, bushy eyebrows straining under the weight of his creased forehead.

"And we have important work to do," I continued. "For *Project Validation*."

Grandpa's eyes lit up at that. Back in familiar territory. We'd been working on Project Validation since I was six years old. Project goals included proving that Grandpa Walt was telling the truth about meeting an alien thirty years ago and that Dad's been super wrong by not being on board with the whole project from the start.

I . . . might not have told Grandpa about that second part.

Today was the first day of summer vacation. Prime time to work on Project Validation, and nothing—not visitation rules or disapproving dads—was going to stand in the way.

A lively knock sounded at Grandpa's door before it swung open and a hand patted the wall to flip on the living-room light. The hulking figure in the doorway grinned down at me.

"Lemon!" Sully, Grandpa's best friend, bellowed as he strode into the room. He and Grandpa made quite the pair in what I secretly thought of as their Old Man Uniforms. Lumpy blue-gray sweater, khaki pants, and a well-worn pair of house slippers. They could almost be twins except for the fact that Sully was a foot taller and bald as an egg.

Grandpa Walt had known Sully for years before he moved into the home. It had made the change easier and cheered him up to see a familiar face on arrival back in October. So much so that he looped Sully in on Project Validation.

Unfortunately, Sully wasn't the most subtle team member.

"Checking in with Team Greeeeeenie and reporting for duty." He knocked off a salute. "What's on the agenda today?"

"Sully, it's awesome to have your help, but seriously, please," I begged. "A little quieter?"

He slapped a hand over his mouth and gave me a thumbs-up.

"Also," I couldn't help adding, "it's Project Validation."

"Ah, you're no fun," he said, laughing when I rolled my eyes. "Now, spill. What's the plan?"

"Well," I said. "Considering Nurse Edie's out front . . ."

"Right." Sully snapped his fingers. "I'll go take watch," he said, heading for the door. "You can count on me, Team Greeee—"

"Thank you, bye-bye." I herded him the rest of the way out.

Grandpa chuckled as he leaned over his cane. "What about the rest of Team Greeeeeenie?"

"Don't you start too!" A team of goofballs. "The rest of *Project Validation* will be getting our plan in place so we can make the most of the next few weeks."

"Let's hop to it then!" Grandpa Walt said, and I answered his grin with a huge one of my own.

Time to find our aliens.

We had our system down to a science—everything in its proper secret hiding place.

Grandpa Walt reached under his chair cushion to pull out a pile of folders, stuffed to bursting with notes. I flipped over the large landscape painting on the wall to reveal a heavily marked-up map of the town on the back.

Now for the crown jewel of our investigation.

Zipping into the bedroom, I paused at the bedside table, patting hello to Grandpa's favorite garden gnome statue and the framed photo of Grandma Frannie. Grandpa Walt always said I was the spitting image of Grandma, and it was nice to see the proof in the pictures since she died before I was born. Same wavy light brown hair that never quite knew how to stay put. Same short legs. Same rosy white skin and crooked smile.

Same determination to help Grandpa Walt prove himself.

I shared a grin with her as I crouched to reach under the

bed for our hefty Project Validation master binder—

Only to come up empty.

Weird.

Flattening to the ground, I peered into the dark space and got a face full of dust bunnies, balled-up socks, and a whole lot of nothing else where a binder should be.

"Hey, Grandpa," I called as I righted myself and stuck my head through the doorway. "Where's the binder?"

"Hmm?" He didn't look up, busy sorting through the folders in his lap.

"Grandpa." I stepped over and waved a hand in front of his face to get his attention. "Where'd you put the binder? It's not under the bed."

"Sure it is." He frowned, cutting a look across the room. "Isn't it?"

"Nope." I rocked back on my heels and blew out a breath. This wasn't our first time at the 'Where'd Grandpa Walt Stash It?' rodeo, and fortunately, there were only so many places for a two-inch-thick binder to hide. After five minutes of rooting around, I finally found it in the cupboard under the bathroom sink.

"Got it," I hollered. Tugging the binder free, I hauled it over and plopped it down on the coffee table. "Whew! We're gonna have to split this thing into two soon!"

"Where was it?" Grandpa Walt eyed the binder suspiciously.

"In the bathroom," I said with a laugh. "I'm not even going to ask."

"Hmpf," he grunted before shaking his head. "Anyhow, you found it, so let's get started."

"Okay." I grabbed the binder, flipping to the last page. "Last summer, we searched the woods by quadrants visually and with the metal detector, to minimal results."

"The change jar begs to differ on minimal results," Grandpa Walt said, twitching his chin at the bookshelf, where the half-full jar sat in a place of pride among his garden gnome collection.

"Fair, but still not the results we're looking for. Also, I've been downloading the SETI activity reports," I said, pulling pages out of my pocket from the institute for the Search for Extraterrestrial Intelligence. "But . . . not much news there either. And nothing in the usual forums—at least, not for our area." A frankly annoying lack of tips to start our summer with.

"I'm not going to be much help, considering my bum hip," he said.

"No worries," I reassured him. "I'll do the legwork and come back with regular updates."

"Your father—"

"I'll figure out how to work around Dad. Been doing that for years." One of my many well-honed skills.

"Lemon." Grandpa Walt spoke gently as he set the files on the coffee table. He rubbed at his forehead, mouth turned down in thought. "I hate getting between you and your father like this. I don't want you two ending up like . . . well, like me and him."

"You're not doing anything. Dad's the one with the problem. Him and his lifetime membership on Team Denial."

"It's been *thirty* years. Maybe it's time to start being realistic."

Nope. No way. Time to nip that doubt in the bud. "Was it *realistic* for people to think they could travel to the moon? What if they'd thought, 'You know, that's pretty far and we don't have enough snacks, want to stay home?' Where would we be then? Hmm?" I shook my head. "We can't give up. Not yet."

"I'm getting tired." Grandpa Walt sighed, sagging back in his chair. He did look tired. His scraggly hair was a bit wild and his glasses were smudged. He wasn't young, not at seventy-two, but he was starting to look *old*. The papery, fragile kind of old.

I hated it.

"Tell me the story," I said. If there was anything that could turn this day around . . .

"Lemon—"

"Just tell me the story," I pleaded before flying to the bookshelf. Grabbing the nearest gnome statue, I looked over at Grandpa. He stuffed a pillow behind himself and sat up a little straighter. Progress. I nipped back and sat on the ratty old cushioned stool. "Come on," I said, wiggling the gnome at him. "One more time."

He let out a long breath before laughing quietly. "Okay," he said, with the grin that never changed. The one that was just for me. The one from all of my best memories.

"It was a hot summer night. Hotter than it had any right to be, but that's the weather for you. Turns out, it wasn't the least predictable thing to happen that evening." Grandpa bopped me on the nose as I mouthed the words along with him. "Frannie was home putting your dad to bed, and I was in charge of the new pup. A birthday present for your father."

He chuckled to himself. "Ugliest little mutt you'd ever seen, but a good dog. I was out walking him for his second nightly run—piles of energy, that one—and we took a path through the woods. That's when it happened."

"There was a whooshing sound. Louder than any wind," I said, leaning forward. This was my favorite part. When the magic happened. "A big gust of air came and the ground vibrated, almost knocking you off your feet."

Grandpa Walt nodded along. "Never saw what caused it,

and I went back with the dog three nights in a row trying to figure it out. On the third night—"

"You found her—"

"She found *me*," he said. "I tripped in the dark and fell into a stream. Looked up to see a little green face, asking me if I was okay."

"Gnemo," I whispered. My Grandpa Walt meeting a real live alien.

"Can still see her face clear as day." His eyes went misty at the memory. "I thought I was hallucinating. Pointy hat, big eyes, maybe three feet tall . . . she looked like an overgrown garden gnome. Which was impossible!"

"Except," I prompted.

"The green skin and the strange technology." He shook his head. "She was an alien. Unimaginable as it seemed. But then again—"

"How could we know what aliens look like?" I chimed in.

Grandpa nodded. "Maybe it was the plumber in me," he said. "I'd already seen some strange things in my life and had a hard time denying what was right in front of my face."

"Plus the dog liked her," I said.

"Plus the dog liked her," he agreed. "Really, Gnemo was so friendly, I didn't even have a chance to be scared. We talked for hours about Earth and space and everything that's out there.

One night, and galaxies opened up to me. It was incredible."

I could picture it perfectly. Grandpa and his alien, sitting under the stars, chatting about the universe. I'd never want to let an experience like that go either.

"And then . . ." Grandpa trailed off.

"Gnemo had to go back to her ship, and Grandma almost divorced you for getting home so late," I finished for him.

"Still surprised she didn't with everything that came after," Grandpa said. "Frannie was one of a kind."

"She *believed* you," I said, taking his weathered hand in mine. "She always did, and I do too. Do you think she'd want us to give up?"

Grandpa Walt's gaze flitted sideways at the bedroom before turning to me. "Frannie said . . ." He stopped to clear his throat. "Now that we know they're out there, we have to let them know they're always welcome back. 'Leave the door open,' she said." Grandpa squeezed my hand. "I think she'd be pretty peeved if we let it shut."

"Yes!" I pumped my fist in the air. "Okay—"

A loud cough from the doorway cut me off. Sully stood there sheepishly. "Hey, gang, incoming," he said. "Sorry, they caught me by surprise."

They? I set the gnome statue on the table and jumped to my feet.

Nurse Edie elbowed past Sully, crisp scrubs swooshing as she marched into the room. She glared down the narrow blade of her nose at me. Effective, but not as piercing as the one from the man behind her. The one whose shoulders were set in a disappointed slope I was keenly familiar with.

I waved weakly. "Heeeeeeeeeeeey, Dad."

CHAPTER 2

Nurse Edie rubbed at her temples. I wasn't sorry for the Lemon-flavored headache she had brewing. She had called my *dad*.

Without even a heads-up!

"Lemon," she began, mouth set in a stern line.

"You know, I'm almost twelve," I pointed out. "Old enough to get a library card on my own, which is a lot of responsibility and should qualify me for visits after six. I'm just saying."

Edie and Dad exchanged looks. "Mr. Peabody," she said as she moved to hustle Sully out the door. "I trust you'll review the rules with your daughter?"

"Yes, ma'am," Dad agreed before turning back to me.

"See you for bingo tomorrow, Walt!" Sully called from the hall, and Grandpa waved before the door closed.

A muscle in Dad's jaw ticked as he looked around the room, and I became painfully aware of how much Project Validation material was in sight.

It wasn't that he didn't know what we were working on so much as he never wanted to see or hear about it. Ever.

I quietly tried to hide the folders behind my back, wincing as a paper fluttered to the floor. We all watched it fall.

Dad took a steadying breath and turned to Grandpa. "Walter," he said with a nod.

"Patrick." Grandpa gave him a short nod in return.

And then no one. Said. *Anything.*

May I present Dad and Grandpa, everyone. Tied for first place at the Awkward Olympics from here until the end of time. Thank goodness they had me.

"Good to see you, son," I said, dropping my voice a few octaves in a faux growl. "You too, Dad. Been a while."

Grandpa stifled a snort as Dad sighed. It was forever weird when I saw them side by side like this. Dad was basically a younger clone of Grandpa, with the same bushy eyebrows and the same weird cowlick that could never be tamed.

Same ridiculous stubborn streak too.

As another beat of awkward silence stretched, I thought I

was going to have to jump in again with some lines about the weather or local sports. But Grandpa finally spoke up instead.

"It *is* good to see you, Patrick," he said.

"Been keeping busy?" Dad asked, glancing over at the Project Validation binder on the table. He stiffened when he saw the green gnome statue beside it.

Then he gave himself a shake and pulled a newspaper clipping out of his pocket. "Brought your sudoku," he said, handing it to Grandpa. "It's a good one this week."

Grandpa frowned as he took it. "Only just started the last one you brought me. Give a man a few days to puzzle it out."

"That's from last Saturday, Walter," Dad said softly.

The lines returned full force to Grandpa Walt's forehead. "They say time flies when you're having fun," I said, poking at his shoulder. "I guess that could apply to sudoku."

Grandpa chuckled half-heartedly, staring at the paper in his hand until Dad cleared his throat.

"The nurses said you've had a pretty good week. If we keep to your routine"—a pointed look at me—"hopefully that trend will continue."

"I'm glad Edie's keeping you informed," Grandpa said dryly. "I'm sure you'll update me if there's anything *I* need to know."

"You don't listen to what you're told anyway," Dad said.

"Nobody tells me anything reasonable," Grandpa snarked.

"That's not—" Dad dragged a hand over his face as he cut himself off.

Like clockwork. The chitchat collapsed into an argument every time.

"I'm not here to fight," Dad said. "Just to check in and pick up Lemon." He rapped his knuckles against the table. "You seem to be in fine form, so we'll head out. Lemon, get this stuff put away and I'll meet you in the hall."

"See you, Patrick," Grandpa called as Dad strode out the door, earning a grunt in reply.

Different visit, same ending. Dad couldn't stand to be here longer than five minutes.

At Grandpa's old house, Dad would let me stay on my own for at least a few hours. Longer, if I had time to negotiate. We got loads of work done.

But now, backed up by nursing staff and visiting hours, there was no discussion. No checking to see if *I* was done chatting with Grandpa. I was tired of it.

Something had to change. Soon.

I took my time putting everything back in its proper place and giving Grandpa a hug goodbye. "Love you to the moon and more," I whispered in his ear.

He squeezed me back. "Love you too, sweetie."

Dad tried to steer me down the hall to the front door as soon as I came out. I pushed back at his insistent nudges, making sure to smile and wave at different residents.

He could rush me all he wanted, but this was important too. Making connections.

Visiting Grandpa here was never going to be like it was when he was at home. Not with the horrendously ugly carpet, lingering smell of cleaning products and old potatoes, and the fact that he had a pile of other elderly strangers as housemates. The first two things I couldn't change.

As for the third . . . slowly but surely, the strangers were becoming friends, and Grandpa liked to say the rest was only window dressing. We were making it a new kind of home.

Despite Dad's grouchiness.

We reached the car, and he gestured for me to get in. The door slammed shut, popping my little bubble of Grandpa time, and I buckled up, braced for a lecture.

"We will talk about this at home with your mother," was all he said.

Honestly, I could give it to myself at this point.

The rules are in place for a reason, Lemon.

You need to respect the restrictions of your grandfather's new situation.

He doesn't need you riling him up.

Not that me reciting it from heart would slow Dad down. He'd take it as a sign to add new points. Maybe a quiz.

We turned toward our street, and something caught my eye when we pulled up to a stop sign. I peered through the evening light, trying to get a better glimpse of the little gray house on the corner. Was that? Oooh. It *was*.

"Lemon," Dad bit out. "Quit fidgeting. What are you looking at?"

I knew the instant he saw it. Dad's face got all pinched as he sucked in a breath, his knuckles going white on the steering wheel. He stepped on the gas, and I craned my neck to get one last look at the new garden gnome sitting proudly in Mrs. Harrison's front yard.

I shouldn't have looked so obviously. I should have pretended not to see anything and waited to get a good look at it on my own tomorrow.

But its little green face called to me.

One of Patrick Peabody's big-time rules: don't acknowledge the garden gnomes. Hard to obey when they were literally all over town. Except for our house, of course.

It wasn't like they were hurting anyone. People were just having fun, but Dad counted it as another injustice to hold against Grandpa Walt. Because Grandpa's in charge of everyone else in Linleydale, I guess.

Pssh.

Although it was a little his fault.

After he met the alien, he told a friend who told a friend who told another friend, and it became a thing. A minor local legend. Then someone gave Grandpa a garden gnome with a painted green face, and *that* caught on. It's sort of a tradition now for people to have green gnomes in their gardens. Half of them probably didn't even know *why* it was a thing. They just did it because it's fun.

And it is!

But *I* knew why they did it.

And *Dad* knew why.

And he got reminded every time we drove through town, which was why I wasn't supposed to be looking at them. That was probably going to be added to the lecture.

Blergh.

Dad pulled into the drive and quickly made his way across our ornament-free lawn. I followed. The sooner he gave me his aliens-aren't-real speech, the sooner I could get back to Project Validation.

"You know, now would be a really great time to show up," I whispered to the universe. "Pretty sure a UFO appearance would distract from my grounding."

I looked up. Not even a funky-looking cloud on the horizon.

"Lemon," my dad called from the doorway. "*What* are you doing? Come inside."

Any time now, little green buddies.

I shook my head.

What's the holdup?

Gnedley

Shrieking alarms blared as Gnedley frowned at the flashing lights of his console.

"Join the Alliance," they'd said.

"See the universe," they'd said.

No one mentioned the part where your ship could explode in the middle of space.

Another warning bell joined the screaming pitch, and Gnedley fought the urge to cover his ears. Point made. Everyone was well aware of their imminent death, *thank you very much*.

"Captain." Chief Gneelix's voice crackled through the comms. "We've lost another power cell. The core's overheating. She can't take much more of this!"

Neither could Gnedley.

"Reroute power from secondary systems," Captain Gnemo ordered, bracing herself against the arm of her chair as the ship pulsed around them.

"I'm already patching the patches, Captain. Any more stress and—" Gneelix produced a long, drawn-out crashing noise.

"Thank you, Chief," Captain Gnemo said, cutting Gneelix off. "The severity of the situation has been noted." Captain Gnemo stared silently at her monitor as the steady whine of the alarms continued to beat across the bridge.

Every passing second felt like a step toward destruction. *Would* they explode? Or simply lose power? Left to drift through space with no way to escape, no way to call for help—

"Ensign Gnedley." He jumped at the captain's voice. "What's our closest landing site?" she asked, keeping her eyes on the data whizzing by on her screen.

Closest landing site. Right. Gnedley could acquire that information. Easily. He stared at the console in front of him.

Why were there so many buttons?

"Ensign. Breathe," Captain Gnemo said, leaning intently toward him. "That's not a request."

Gnedley sucked in air as he peered at his screen.

"Remember your training," the captain continued. "You know what to do."

"And it would be great if you could do it before our horrible deaths," Gneelix added.

Captain Gnemo smacked a hand down, muting the comms before nodding at Gnedley.

Yes. His training. He could do this.

After a few failed attempts, Gnedley pulled up the map, checking the list of approved sites. Captain Gnemo grimaced when he told her the nearest one.

"Too far," Commander Gnilsson chimed in. The first officer, who had been quietly working through his own calculations, leaned over to look at Gnedley's results. "We'll never make that. Nothing's closer?"

Gnedley swiveled his monitor to display the list. "IC 525-1 is considerably closer, but—"

"It's been taken off our route," Commander Gnilsson finished for him grimly. "Restricted access." He scratched a hand through his short beard before turning to the captain. "We won't make it any farther," he said. "It looks like 525-1 is our only option for a safe landing."

The comms squealed as Gneelix cut back in. "All I need is solid ground and a few hours to work on this trash heap in peace."

"A plan is in the works, Gneelix," Captain Gnemo assured her. "Stand by."

"Got nowhere else to go," Gneelix muttered. "Escape pods are busted too."

The captain pinched the bridge of her nose before addressing Gnedley. "Open a channel to HQ," she said. "We need clearance for the change in route."

Commander Gnilsson frowned. "Captain, by the time—"

"We're doing this by the book," she asserted with finality.

Gnedley struggled to navigate his console as the ship rumbled and heaved, although a fair amount of the shaking seemed to stem from his own fingers. *Focus, Gnedley.* Everything was shuddering so erratically it took him a moment to recognize the error message in front of him. "Captain, external communications are down. I can't get through."

She cursed, slapping her own screen. The ship groaned and tilted to the left, nearly sending everyone to the floor.

This was it. Gnedley's first mission would be his last.

"We need to land *now*," Gneelix shouted. "Unless the plan is to do it more delicately in tiny little pieces spread throughout the atmosphere."

"Gnilsson," Gnemo barked. "Chart a course for IC 525-1. We'll worry about clearance after we land. Gneelix, give us as much power as you can."

"How?" Chief Gneelix was almost drowned out by clangs from the belly of the ship. "Should I get out and push?"

"You're telling me the *Gnar Five* is well and truly done? She's got nothing left?" Captain Gnemo shot back at the speaker.

"Nothing left . . . ," Gneelix sputtered. "Stand by, Captain." The ship gave a mighty roar as Gneelix got to work.

"Hold steady, everyone," Captain Gnemo said, bracing herself against the arms of her chair. "Take us down, Gnilsson."

The first officer smirked at Gnedley as his fingers flew over the controls. "Better strap in, sprout," he said. "We'll be coming in rough."

Gnedley tightened his seat belt, swallowing hard.

CHAPTER 3

The suspense was killing me.

I got one foot through the door when Mom appeared out of nowhere, holding up a finger before Dad could open his mouth. She was in her comfy leggings, with her sandy blond hair tied up in a messy bun, but her face was all business.

"Discussions wait until after dinner," she declared, leaving no room for arguments. "We won't get anywhere on empty stomachs."

I set the table as Dad helped finish cooking, and all three of us sat down to eat. Mushing the peas around my plate, I snuck a look at my parents, who were happily chatting about whether or not the lawn could wait to be cut. The lawn! Like I wasn't sitting right there with my stomach doing a deep dive to my toes.

A lecture I could handle. *Anticipation* of a lecture was torture.

How much trouble was I in? Even if I'd skirted Edie's rules, shouldn't wanting to spend time with Grandpa be a *good thing*?

Ugh. Enough was enough.

"I can't take it anymore!" My parents blinked in surprise as I slammed down my fork. "Punish me. Yell at me. Do what you're going to do, but please do it now!"

Mom and Dad shared a look before setting down their own utensils. Finally.

"You're all done with that?" Mom pointed at my plate. "Let's clear the table."

"*Whyyyyyyyyyyyyyy?*" Flinging myself back in my chair, I let my body slide to the floor.

Dad knocked on the table. "Dishwasher's the other way."

I managed to stand with minimal grumbling. Not zero, because I am a human being, thank you very much, but a respectable three on the grumble scale. After setting my dishes in the rack, I shuffled back to the table while Mom made a cup of tea—boiled the kettle and everything tea—and then at last, eight hundred hours later, we were ready to discuss.

And yet they stayed silent.

So I kept my mouth shut too, counting the freckles that

stood out on Mom's fair-skinned hands as she warmed them around her mug.

The clock ticked.

The sink gurgled.

This was silly. Someone should start us on the right foot. Set a levelheaded tone. "I understand you may feel the need to ground me," I began.

"And what would we be grounding you for?" Mom asked, chin cupped in one hand, elbow resting on the table.

Red alert. Major trap.

"Well, if you're not sure, you should gather all the facts before doling out punishments. How about we revisit this once you've had time to investigate further?" I started inching out of my seat but froze when Dad cleared his throat.

"Lemon," he said. "You know exactly where this conversation needs to begin."

I widened my eyes and held his stare. This is not the issue you're looking for. Move on from this topic—yeah, that totally wasn't working.

"Why did you tell us you were going to Marlo's this afternoon?" Dad asked with a frown. "You know how we feel about lying."

Oh, right. That. "I *did* go to Marlo's." One hundred percent not a lie. "I just decided to stop by Grandpa's on the way home."

Dad crossed his arms. "Marlo lives next door."

"I took the scenic route! It's summer! Vitamin D!"

Mom smothered a laugh and shook her head. "Sweetie," she said, schooling her face back into a serious gaze. "Any way you twist it, you still told us one thing and did another. You have to be up front about what you're doing and where you're going. We need to be able to trust you."

"Why can't you trust me to visit Grandpa whenever I want?" Because let's be honest, that's the real issue here.

"We discussed this when your grandfather moved into the retirement home." Dad rubbed at the deep crease in his forehead. "It's not like it was at his house. They have rules—"

"Dumb rules."

"That we have to follow," he continued, ignoring me. Not unusual. Always annoying. "Even though you might not agree with them, their rules are in place for a reason, and we have to respect that. More importantly, you can't rile up your grandfather and the other residents."

The talking points! Right on cue. "Who was I riling? There was no riling." Rallying, maybe. Inspiring? I mean, one could hope.

"Remember when Grandpa was diagnosed? All of the information we got from the Alzheimer's Society? We talked about how things would have to change." Mom spoke gently, like this was breaking news and not something they'd been hammering into me for months already. My stomach clenched just as hard as it had the *first* time we talked about it.

"Okay, but I didn't think you meant when I could see him and how I was supposed to visit with him. You keep piling on the restrictions." It was beginning to look like their endgame was me not seeing Grandpa at all. Which was just—no.

"Again, for a *reason*." Dad scowled as he leaned back in his chair. "Because, Lenore—"

I swallowed the hiss that nearly escaped. "It's not Lenore, it's *Lemon*."

"Your *name* is Lenore," he corrected. "You can't go by that nickname forever."

A nickname he only hated because Grandpa gave it to me.

"Pretty sure I can," I muttered.

"It's not good for either one of you when you go and get him excited," Dad pressed on. "Excited leads to agitated and confused." He stared at a spot over my shoulder, eyes unfocused.

"You haven't experienced that yet. I have," he said softly. "I don't want you to see a bad episode if we can avoid it. But the bad episodes are going to turn into bad days. And then . . . we'll have another chat when that time comes." He trailed off, rubbing at a mysterious stain on the table, and Mom reached out to squeeze his shoulder.

"We don't want to stop you from seeing your grandpa," she said. "But we need to work together and compromise if we're going to make this situation work for everyone."

That sounded like a convoluted way of saying stop arguing and do what we say. "What's the compromise?"

"You're on summer vacation, and you have a lot of time on your hands." Mom paused at the look on my face.

My schedule was *jam-packed*. Grandpa and I had piles of work to do, and then there was hanging out with Marlo. A lot of time? What?

"You can't spend it all with Grandpa Walt," Mom said firmly. "You can spend some of it," she hurried on before I could protest. "That's part of the compromise, okay? We know you want to see him." She looked over at Dad, who nodded reluctantly.

"Mornings or afternoons. Not evenings," he said. "And listen to Edie. She's the boss."

"Okay." Irritating, but I could work with that. "What else?" Because there had to be more. This was way too easy.

"We want you to pick an activity." Mom jumped up to grab her tablet from the living room. "There's tons going on in town this summer, and we want you to get involved."

Oh, here it comes. . . .

She set the tablet on the table and swiped at the screen,

bringing a slew of saved tabs to life. "You can't spend the whole summer hunting aliens." Mom shot a quick look at Dad as he abruptly got up from his chair.

"It's a search, not a hunt," I said automatically, flipping through the tabs.

"Take a look." She tapped at the side of the tablet. "Talk to Marlo. If she's interested, we can discuss it with Sofía and Allison and sign you up together. Might be good to get out there and make some more friends."

"Why would Marlo and I need more friends? We're awesome. Also . . ." I waved a hand at the options before me. "Volleyball camp? Recreational soccer league? *Swim team?* Who's this imaginary child you're picking activities for? She's very athletic."

Dad sat back down with a glass of water and a heavy sigh. "Let me put it this way," he said. "You pick or we'll pick for you."

I scooped up the tablet. "Yup, I'm sure I can find something great in here. Summer fun. Exciting times." Backing out of the kitchen, I jerked a thumb over my shoulder. "Going to my room so I can read through and weigh my choices. Make an informed decision."

"Sounds good," Mom said. "Oh, and Lemon?" She stopped me in my tracks with a narrow stare punctuated by a wicked grin. "You're on garbage duty for the next month," she said.

"No more fibbing about where you're going and what you're up to. Understood?"

I nodded and escaped upstairs, taking the steps two at a time. Once the door was firmly shut behind me, I let out a deep breath and tossed the tablet onto my bed. What a day. Not the *best* start to summer, but not a total bust either.

Picking my way over the clothes and things strewn across the floor, I collapsed into a velvety green chair stashed in the corner. One of the treasures I'd rescued from Grandpa Walt's house when he moved out. It had a deep cushion and a high back with sides that stuck out like little wings. The perfect chair to lounge in and plot. I also had a colorful rag rug from the spare room I always slept over in. Pretty sure Grandma Frannie made it. It was a bit faded, but it really tied the room together.

A few other knickknacks littered my shelves and bookcase. Things Grandpa couldn't fit into his new place. Dad claimed he didn't want any of it, and I couldn't bring myself to let them get thrown out. Part of me felt silly, especially when Dad went on about how it was only *stuff*. To be honest, my room was seriously crowded now. But every time I went to get rid of something, a little twist in my heart traveled up my throat and said *not yet*.

I'd never tell Dad, but I also wanted to keep it all in case it helped Grandpa down the line. When he'd need all the memories he could get.

Alzheimer's disease, Mom and Dad called it. Or Old Timer's, as Grandpa liked to say. From what they'd told me and what I'd researched on my own, it's . . . not good. There's no cure. I didn't like to think about that or what it was going to do to Grandpa.

What it was doing right now.

There was no way for me to fight that.

But today—this summer—for the next however long we had left, I could spend time with Grandpa and work on Project Validation. Prove Grandpa right and maybe . . . actually fix things between him and Dad. If I could show him that Grandpa hasn't been lying all these years, he couldn't stay mad at him, right?

And in order to work on Project Validation, I had to deal with this alternate activity business. I reached over and snagged the tablet. Clicking on tab after tab, I rolled my eyes at the sheer amount of sports ball my parents were determined to set me up with. There had to be *something* I could sign up for and immediately ditch. I froze as one page leaped out.

It was *perfect*. Did Mom even know she had tagged this? She must not have realized. . . .

Was she secretly in favor of Project Validation?

No. No way. It had to be a mistake.

Too late now! She'd made the list, and I had the freedom to choose. This was happening. Sure, parents, I'll broaden my interests. Broaden them until I circle back around to my original goal. I cackled in my glorious green chair. See? So good for plotting.

With a bit more planning and Marlo on board, there wouldn't be much standing in my way. I stood up for a satisfying stretch. After switching off the light, I flopped onto my bed and watched my glow-in-the-dark constellations come to life. Some were real. The rest were me imagining where Grandpa's aliens could live.

I'd spent so many nights lying in bed, still mostly dressed and ready to head out at the first sign of their return. This was going to be the summer. I could feel it.

And now, more than ever—I was ready.

Whoooosh.

I bolted upright in bed, wiping drool off my chin as I shook the sleep out of my brain. *What was that?* Straining my ears, all I could hear was the soft patter of rain on the roof. It must've been a dream.

Except . . .

I couldn't shake the feeling that there'd been *something*. Sleep would be impossible unless I checked. Flipping back the covers, I hopped out of bed and went to my window. Drops of rain streamed down the glass. The backyard was barely visible through the dark, let alone the woods beyond.

A flash of light cut through the sky.

Lightning?

Whooosh.

That definitely wasn't thunder.

My heart pounded as I pulled up the window and pressed my face against the screen. You're overreacting, Lemon. It's a summer storm. Nothing to get excited about.

But there—another flash over the woods. A whirring buzz grew louder and louder. Squinting against the dark, I could make out bits of the forest under the light of the moon.

I didn't want to breathe. Didn't want to move in case I broke the spell that was building.

A huge shadow streaked across the sky, blocking out the moon before a faint *whump* sounded and a few trees shook sideways.

Oh.

My.

"What?" I gasped. Breathe. Breathe, Lemon. Holy moly, oh my goodness, *breathe.*

Something had definitely gone down in Linleydale Woods.

In the middle of the night. With no one around.

This could be it. Them. The aliens. It was happening exactly like Grandpa Walt had described. I *had* to go check. For his sake. And mine. And Dad's. Who knew how long they'd be there for? What if I missed out?

Grabbing clothes off the floor, I stuffed them inside my

covers in a loglike shape and fluffed up the pillow. I stepped back to examine the effect. It was Lemon-ish. Someone poking their head in my door probably wouldn't question it.

I slipped on my gym shoes and an extra hoodie and then dug through my desk.

Flashlight. Check. Phone. Check. Notebook. Check.

That seemed like the basics of an alien search expedition. I snagged a small fold-up bag from the back of my door and stuffed everything inside.

Now. Escape my house without detection. That was the trick.

Going downstairs meant risking the creaky landing and the squeaky step. I couldn't think of any other—oh! Sliding open the bottom desk drawer, I rifled through until I found what I was looking for.

Aha. *Lemon's Emergency Escape Plan to Be Used in Case of Fire or Other Such Emergencies. Created by Marlo and Lemon. For Emergencies.*

Perfect.

For emergencies only, Lemon! Marlo's voice scolded in my head.

"Which this totally is," I argued. My chance to find Grandpa's aliens was textbook emergency, in my opinion.

I clicked the lock on the window screen and slid it back

gently, keeping an ear out for roaming parents. So far, so good. I reviewed Marlo's diagram before sticking it in my pocket.

Okay, emergency plan. Show me what you've got.

Supplies secure in the bag looped around my wrist, I carefully made my way through the window and onto the roof. The rain made everything slick, but I took a firm grasp on my handholds and inched toward the edge. From there, I slid onto my butt so I could wiggle down to the garage roof. I scooted across and dropped down the garden wall before plopping on the ground.

Wow.

That actually worked.

Of course it did, Marlo's voice snapped again. *I make great plans. Now go back inside, because* your *plans are terrible.*

"No can do," I whispered. "The mission has begun." Running to the end of our backyard, I kept low to the ground until I reached our fence, using the latticework to climb up and over. Into the woods we go.

The rain dripped through the trees as I lifted my hood to cover my already half-soaked hair. I squinted through the darkness, trying to find a clear path. The shadows were deeper inside the woods as branches and leaves stretched to filter out the moonlight.

I dug the flashlight out of my bag and turned it on, the

broad beam lighting up the forest floor. Safety first.

The question now was where to start. Grandpa Walt and I had been over every stick of the Linleydale Woods, and there were only so many clearings big enough for a spaceship. I headed in the direction of one of the first spots he'd shown me—the spot where he suspected they'd landed last time. Maybe I'd be lucky.

Despite the rain sliding down my neck and my soggy shoes slurping through the mud, I couldn't keep the smile off my face. I, Lemon Peabody, could be meeting aliens *tonight*.

I ducked under a branch, nearly face planting as another one came out of nowhere. First things first—make it there in one piece. It'd be too easy to get turned around in the dark. Slowing down a bit, I picked my way through the undergrowth, looking for familiar signs along the way.

The fallen tree with the fluffy moss growing on one end.

The clump of rocks I thought was a fairy house when I was a kid.

The waving light up ahead.

Wait a minute.

I flicked off my flashlight and ducked behind the nearest tree. Sure enough, there was Grandpa's clearing, and through the trees and the rainy mist, I could see the steady beam of at least three lights.

Time to bring the stealth. I crouched, keeping my steps as quiet as I could, traveling serpentine to the edge of the clearing. Squatting behind the largest tree, I risked a peek—

And gasped at the sight of a genuine spaceship right there in front of me in the middle of the woods.

It looked darkish gray . . . although that could have been the smoke drifting out from a few separate locations. The whole thing was smaller than I thought it'd be. Hard to judge when it was zooming through the dark. Fins curved out on either side, framing the large window at the front. Movement caught my eye as a ramp lowered from the rear. Two—no, three figures emerged.

I should get closer. I should go over there, introduce myself, tell them about Grandpa.

You don't even know that those are your aliens.

I snarled at the return of Marlo's voice. It's aliens! In our woods! Who else would they be, *Marlo*?

Literally anyone.

That was . . . an annoyingly good point. As much as I wanted to barrel over, I really didn't know what I was walking into. Somehow actually seeing the ship and the aliens, even from a distance, made this whole thing more real. I shouldn't go alone.

At least I'd confirmed they were here. This was the most

progress Project Validation had made . . . *ever*! I couldn't wait to tell Grandpa and Marlo.

Oh! Proof! They might think this was some sort of bananas dream I'd had otherwise. I dug through my bag for my phone and unlocked it.

Despite the rain and my shaking hands, I managed to get a few good pictures of the ship and the shadowy figures. Then I brought up my GPS to pin the location. Just in case.

There. Proof and a map.

I slunk back into the woods, waiting until I was far enough away to turn on my flashlight. I lasted about three more steps before I started running. Slipping and sliding through the mud, I couldn't stop laughing. This was it. In one night, we'd skipped ahead to phase three—no, phase *four*!—of Project Validation. I had so many things to do. I needed to—Marlo! I had to update her.

Pulling my phone back out, I checked the time.

She would probably prefer that update in about seven hours.

No worries. I had plenty to prepare in the meantime.

Including . . . what did you even put in a Welcome to Earth basket?

Gnedley

Gnedley stared at the loading bay doors, scrunching the hem of his shirt in his hands.

They'd made it.

The *Gnar Five* had landed—in essentially one piece—on IC 525-1, and now here he was. On an alien world. The very reason he'd become a full-fledged member of the Interplanetary Natural Archives Alliance in the first place. His dream come true.

Gnedley gulped.

One should never be too hasty in achieving their dreams. He smoothed out the red fabric of his uniform and tugged his hat firmly onto his head. A chat with the captain was in order. Gnedley could undoubtedly still assist the crew from *inside* the ship.

Before he could turn back, the bay doors swung open and strong hands pushed Gnedley from behind. He stumbled down the ramp as it lowered and found himself standing in the rain inside a darkened clearing.

"Well, Ensign?" Gneelix called from the doorway. "Is there air on this planet?"

Air? *Air?*

Wasn't that something to confirm *before* landing? Gnedley's brain flipped through every file he'd read on 525-1 and drew a blank. He gasped, dimly aware of water drizzling down his neck, trying to steady his breath—no! Why did he do that? Don't breathe it *in*! Gnedley expelled all the air from his chest, scraping at his tongue.

This was how he'd die.

Not exploding in space, but guzzling poisonous alien atmosphere to his doom. "Ensign." Captain Gnemo's voice cut through his panic and Gneelix's laughter. "If you'll recall, the Alliance has been to 525-1 before," she said, taking pity on him. "It's safe to breathe, I assure you."

"Oh, yes, of course, Captain," Gnedley stammered, feeling a blush streak up his cheeks.

She shot a look at the still snickering Gneelix. "I believe we have a ship to repair?"

Gneelix knocked off a salute and grabbed her toolbox

before heading down the ramp. She bumped shoulders with Gnedley on her way to the underbelly of the ship. "Relax, Ensign," she said. "The *Gnar Five* has survived worse, and so will you."

It was going to get worse?

"Most important rule for IC planets." Captain Gnemo clapped a hand on his shoulder, turning him back around. "Implement standard safety procedures immediately," she said. "Go help Commander Gnilsson set up the perimeter fence, and I'll take first patrol." The captain strode off, leaving Gnedley to locate Gnilsson.

The first officer hadn't strayed far from the ship. "Ah! Gnedley, right on time," he said, fighting to get a gray shield panel to stand up in the muddy ground. "Hold this."

Gnedley trotted over and grabbed the thin metal on either side. The commander's hand flew by his face, whacking a fist down on the flat top of the shield. He grinned, satisfied when it managed to stay in place. "Only thirty-nine more to go!"

They worked in tandem, getting covered in mud and chilled to the bone.

Commander Gnilsson pushed up the sleeve of his purple uniform shirt, smearing his forearm with dirt. "Enjoying the glamorous life of an Alliance crew member so far?"

Gnedley couldn't catch the laugh that escaped and

decided to risk a little honesty at Commander Gnilsson's echoing chuckle. "It's not exactly as I anticipated."

Gnilsson raised a hand to his chest. "What? They didn't put broken-down ships, rugged landscapes, and absolutely terrible food in the training holo?"

"Nothing about the food *at all*," Gnedley groaned.

"Well, if they warned you about that, we'd never get any new sprouts to boss around." Gnilsson patted his belly as it grumbled. "What do you think we'll have for breakfast? Green slime or the orange paste?"

"Is it wrong to hope for the green slime?" Gnedley sighed. If you ate it fast enough, it slid right down your throat. The other stuff tended to . . . stick.

"Hah! See? You're fitting in already," Gnilsson said.

"I'm not sure about that," Gnedley said before he could stop himself.

"If you're talking about Gneelix . . ." The first officer laughed. "She's only happy if she has something to grumble about. Don't take it personally."

"It's not—never mind," Gnedley shook his head, trying not to let his feelings show on his face, but Commander Gnilsson was too perceptive.

"Captain Gnemo?" he guessed. "I know she's a little standoffish, but it's not easy being the leader. Gnemo's had a harder time than most. She's under a lot of pressure, and being *here* isn't helping with that."

Gnilsson clapped his hands together before Gnedley could ask what he meant. "Look at me rambling," he said. "Let's get this going so I can catch some shut-eye before patrol." Retrieving his portable control tablet, Gnilsson logged in a code. The panels buzzed and lights flashed as the array came to life in a dome over their heads. Now their ship was hidden from view and only the crew members with their shield keys could move in and out of the perimeter.

The nearest panel began to vibrate.

"Uh, Commander?" Gnedley pointed the first officer toward the panel currently emitting a high-pitched screech.

"No, you don't!" Gnilsson leaped over and gave it a swift kick, jumping back when sparks flew. The array pulsed once before settling into a quiet hum.

"There we are," he said cheerfully. "You'll learn these little tricks as you go. Some of the older equipment you have to baby, and some of it you have to . . ." He did a slow-motion kick to the side. "It's all in the follow-through."

"Quit abusing our gear!" Gneelix shouted from underneath the ship.

"You're welcome!" Gnilsson yelled back.

"Oh, I say."

Gnedley and Gnilsson looked up at the voice coming from the loading bay door. Doctor Gnog stood at the top of the ramp, their braided beard coming undone, yellow uniform creased, and hat slightly askew. "I had the loveliest nap."

Gnedley looked over at Gnilsson with wide eyes. "I actually forgot they were on the ship," he whispered.

Doctor Gnog squinted at them as the commander laughed. "What did I miss?"

After the good doctor was brought up to speed, Gnedley went to grab a few hours' sleep.

Gneelix too, though she snarled all the way to her bunk. Apparently the ship was in greater disrepair than she'd thought, and their communication system was still down.

They were stranded.

Gnedley had faith that their chief engineer could whip the *Gnar Five* back into shape with her special brand of spit and elbow grease. A necessary skill when your ship was always a breath away from disaster.

The glamorous life of an Alliance crew.

Reaching into his pocket, Gnedley touched the leaf safely hidden there and took some comfort in his token from home.

A home that was now so very far away.

Growing up in the Archives, he'd been surrounded by

stories of exploration and newly encountered species. He watched as every last detail was entered into the catalog. Bit by bit, they were storing the secrets of the universe.

The best reports were from Captain Gnemo. When she wrote about her journeys through the Isolated Communities, Gnedley felt like he was right there with her. He *wished* he was. It was Gnemo's words that had made him realize he was done reading about adventure and ready to go on one.

It wasn't Gnemo's fault that the figure he'd built up in his mind didn't match the one he'd met in real life. Commander Gnilsson had a point. Being a crew member was hard enough. He couldn't imagine what being captain was like.

In any case, he was here now. Despite the near-death experience and the clash of personalities, he couldn't regret his choice. Because . . . living it?

A thousand times better than reading about it.

Except—he shuddered—for the food.

CHAPTER 5

The sun broke through the tree line and beams of light streamed over the neighboring houses. I tucked my legs up on the bed to watch the morning unfold through the window, confident in my plan for the day.

Next to me on the bed, a rumpled pile of blankets shifted as a tousled bunch of blue hair emerged from underneath them. *"Mrpfgh,"* it said.

"Good morning, best friend," I sang, patting the lumpy sheets.

The pile thrashed upright, long limbs flailing. "What?" Marlo's golden cheeks flushed as she rubbed sleep out of her eyes. "Early. *Why?*" She flopped onto her pillow with a moan.

I pulled back the covers. "Because the early bird catches the little green worm."

"Why are you in my room at—" Marlo flung a hand out for her phone to check the time. "It's summer vacation! What's wrong with you? How did you even get in here?"

"Don't be mean when I brought you breakfast." I tossed her a granola bar. Probably should have opened with that. Marlo and mornings were not exactly on speaking terms.

"Seriously, how?" She tore the wrapper with a growl and bit off a chunk.

"Well . . ." I stood up and avoided looking at the window at all costs, but even semi asleep, Marlo was quick on the uptake.

She gulped down her mouthful and crawled out of bed. "Climbing? Again? Mom'll kill you if you hurt her trellis."

"That's why I moved some vines so you can't see the crack unless you're looking for it."

"What?" Marlo pulled open the window screen to stick her head out. "I can't believe you—" She whirled back around. "I should never have shown you the *Marlo's Emergency Escape Plan to Be Used in Case of Fire or Other Such Emergencies*. You *abuse* the knowledge."

Harsh. "Is it 'using' it if I reversed the steps? More an emergency entrance plan in this case. Also," I said, "let me tell you, the trellis is a much better idea on paper than in real life. Gets shakier every time."

"Emergencies only," Marlo hissed.

"If you'll let me explain, I think you'll agree this qualifies."

"*Nnngh.*" Marlo finished off her breakfast and tossed the wrapper onto the side table. She scrubbed a hand over her face. "Okay. I'm awake. Tell me why you broke into my room at rude o'clock in the morning."

"This." I beamed at my very best friend and pointed to the wall behind me. Marlo blinked at the papers, charts, and diagrams covering it from floor to ceiling. I was nothing if not thorough. And considerate. I'd used one of her plain cream-colored walls instead of the purple accent wall. A purple so magnificent we'd vowed never to let anything smother its beauty.

"Oooooh, gosh." Marlo surveyed my solid twenty minutes of sticky-tack-heavy work.

"The good thing," I said, clapping my hands together, "is that I've already worked through the variables on fifty-six different plans, so I know this one is the best."

Theoretically.

Marlo peered at the wall. She turned to stare into my eyes. She looked back at the wall. "Did you sleep at all?"

"Not even a little bit." I flashed her a grin.

"And what exactly is this plan for?" Marlo asked, squinting.

"Project Validation," I said. "It's happening, Marlo. For *real* this time." The celebratory joy bubbling up since last night stopped short at the frown on her face.

"We had a deal. No alien hunting this summer."

"It's a search, not a hunt." I wished people would remember that.

"What happened to Super Chill Summer?" Marlo threw her hands up. "Going to the pool. The Great Popsicle Experiment. Getting as many books as we can carry from the library. Learning how to knit. Working on my book." She pointed at the wall. "*This?* Is not that."

"I get what you're saying," I said. "First things first, I don't want to take away from your writing time. Speaking of—" I reached down and dug through my bag to pull out a notebook. "I read your new draft. Still think you could use a character named Lemon, but it's *so* good. I can't wait to read more." Marlo was the most talented person I knew. Definitely the kind of brains and creativity I wanted on this job.

"Thank you." She grabbed the notebook from me and dropped it on her desk. "And you will. After I write more while you knit and we eat our amazing Popsicles. Guess what's not on that list? Aliens."

"I never said I wasn't going to search for the aliens this summer." I got the words out quickly before she could jump in and argue again. "Hanging out with Grandpa Walt was always on *my* list, which means working on Project Validation."

She took a deep breath, but I kept going. "I know what we

talked about. Especially after last summer."

"It was *not* easy-peasy building a radio tower," she grouched.

"Look how many story ideas you got from that, though! Not the point," I backed off at her glare. "I'm saying those promises were made before."

Marlo lasted a beat before caving. "Before what?"

"Before I had *proof*."

"Okay." Marlo crossed her arms, leaning against her desk. "I'll bite. Explain."

I started with the noises and the lights in the woods. How I snuck out of my house.

"For emergencies only," she hissed again. "It's a simple rule!"

"Do you want to hear this or not?" I waved her off and told her about trekking through the woods to finding the landing spot.

"Question." Marlo held up a finger. "How were you planning on working on Project Validation after you got *murdered in the woods in the middle of the night*?"

"Are you going to let me finish, or are you going to keep interrupting?"

"I'm honestly scared to hear what you did next," she said.

I leaned in, not able to keep the giant smile off my face. "I found them," I said.

"Found *who*?"

"The aliens." I described the ship in the woods and the figures walking around and how I took pictures. She nodded slowly when I mentioned smartening up and heading home to get backup. Marlo-shaped backup, specifically.

I zipped my lips to let her turn it all over in her brain. Sometimes it was best to wait and let Marlo think things through.

"Show me the pictures," she finally said.

I whipped my phone out of my pocket and brought up the shots from last night.

"I don't know what this proves," she said as she swiped along to the end. "It's a bunch of pictures of the woods and some smeary lights and shadows."

"It was raining," I protested. "I promise you. *They were there.*"

"I believe you believe they were there."

"Don't do that," I said. "Don't talk to me like my parents." I pressed a hand to the wall of evidence. "At least let me take you to the landing site."

She hesitated, but it was hard to tell if it was an 'I'm going to give in' pause or an 'I'm figuring out how to let you down' pause.

"Why the big push and all the risk-taking? You've been working on Project Validation for years," she said. "But I've never seen you be this . . . intense."

"I've never been this close before."

Marlo cocked her head to the side, searching my face for the rest of the answer, and I knew I had to give her more.

"It's Grandpa," I said.

She caught my serious-business vibe and moved to sit on her bed, patting the space beside her.

"Going to Shady Elms wasn't only because he was having a hard time managing at home," I said. Marlo and her moms had helped clean up his house for the move. She knew he'd been struggling, but I hadn't let her know how much. We didn't usually keep secrets.

"He was diagnosed with Alzheimer's disease last year," I confessed. "He forgets things. It started out small. He doesn't even know he's doing it half the time, but . . ." Marlo rubbed my back while I swiped at my eyes. "It's getting worse. And I'm scared."

Marlo swept me up in a tight hug. After a moment, she sat back. "Don't take this the wrong way, okay?" she said. "Because that sucks and I'm really sorry it's happening." She took a breath. "If he's getting worse, doesn't it make more sense to spend time with him? Instead of running around for Project Validation?"

"Project Validation is *for* him—"

"I know," Marlo bumped her shoulder against mine. "But he can't go to the woods with you anymore, right? It'll take time away from him to do . . ." She waved a hand at the wall. "All of this."

"I have to." I willed her to understand. "I have to do this for him, Marlo. Before he forgets it was his dream to begin with."

Marlo stared at the intricate display, lips pursed. "Okay," she said.

"Okay?" My cheeks hurt with the grin that split across my face.

"Yes, *but*," Marlo said solemnly. "No more dangerous stuff like sneaking out of your house, okay? Promise me."

"I promise." Nothing could really be considered *dangerous* if I had Marlo along, right?

"Okay then," she said. "Let's do whatever bonkers thing you've come up with."

"I told you, I have the best plan ever."

"Mm-hmm." She stood to poke at some of the sticky notes covering the map of Linleydale Woods. "Does it cover how we're going to get away with searching the woods every day? We're not exactly outdoorsy. You only ever went there with your grandpa, and usually for this kind of stuff. Our parents will get suspicious."

"Not mine," I said. "They decided I need to expand my

interests and pick an activity for the summer. Gave me a list to choose from and everything."

"Really."

"Apparently it's good to get out of the house and make more friends."

Marlo scrunched up her nose. "Why?"

"It's working to our advantage, so whatever." I whipped out the tablet. "One of the things Mom tagged was *this*."

Staring at the website on display, Marlo's brown eyes widened in shock. She shook her head. A little more vehemently than necessary, in my opinion. "No," she said. "Not happening."

"We're never going to get a better opportunity," I said. "This is the *perfect* cover."

"I said I would help, and I meant it." Marlo put her hands on her hips. "But there's got to be another option. There's no way you're talking me into *that*."

"I didn't want to have to do this," I said with regret. Drawing back my shoulders, I placed a hand over my heart. "Marlo García-Reynolds, I hereby call in . . . the Debt."

Marlo took a shaky breath "The Debt? Are you serious?"

"Yes," I said. "The most serious. This is worth it."

"*The*. Debt."

"Is there another one?" I retorted, fully prepared to refresh her memory. "August thirteenth, three years ago. We were having a sleepover."

"I know—"

"The night was clear," I said. "And you were determined to see some stars."

"You're going to do the whole thing." Marlo sighed. "Okay."

"You grabbed your mom's telescope and *broke* it, but I took the blame." A massive act of friendship, if I did say so myself. I ticked off the fallout on my fingers. "I was grounded for three months. I had to pay your mom back."

"I helped."

"Secretly. *And* your mom's never looked at me the same way since." That one hurt. I held up a fourth finger. "I wasn't allowed to come over for *four* months."

"Okay, *fine*," Marlo said, holding her hands up in defeat. "You can call it in. Oh, wow, I already regret this."

"And the Debt shall be repaid," I intoned.

"You're lucky I love you, weirdo." Marlo laughed.

"If you're awake," a voice called up the stairs, "come down for breakfast."

"Yesssssssssss," I said, rubbing my belly. "I'm starving. Do you think I can sweet-talk your mom into making pancakes?" I stuffed my shoes and papers into my bag, pausing over the extensive setup on the wall. "That can wait. Food first."

I trotted down the stairs and Marlo followed behind, muttering.

"Good morning," I said, reaching out to pet Wade, Marlo's gray striped cat, who was lounging in his hammock. He hissed before dropping to the floor and disappearing into the living room. "It's okay," I said. "We'll get there. Not like it's been eight years already." I turned to the kitchen table, pulling out a chair for Marlo and one for myself.

Marlo's mom Allison was at the kitchen island, dressed in her running gear and chopping up red peppers. Her pink hair was pulled back in a high ponytail that bounced along her fair shoulders as she bopped around to the little tune she was humming. Marlo might have inherited her other mom Sofía's curls and golden-beige skin, but her love of bright colors was all Allison. Last week, the pink hair had been mermaid green.

"Love the new do," I grinned.

"Lemon." Allison paused her chopping, doing a double take at my arrival. "How did you—" She stepped into the front hallway and we heard the front door open and close. Allison reappeared, hands on her hips. "Look at that. It still works," she drawled. "I'm hoping the same can be said for my trellis."

"Oh, look! Toast!" I grabbed a quarter piece and stuffed it in my mouth. "Diyiffish."

"So early for this level of shenanigans." Sofía chuckled as

she entered the kitchen, tying off the end of her braid. "Good morning, girls," she said.

"Morning, Mama," Marlo said as Sofía dropped a kiss on her head.

She detoured past the fridge to bring orange juice to the table. "That's quite the load," Sofía said, nudging my bag with her foot. "What have you got in there?"

I swallowed down my mouthful and grinned over at Marlo. "Our summer plans."

Sofía angled her head, making a curious noise as she poured. "And?"

"Tell them the news, Marlo." I bounced in my seat.

She shot me a look before arranging her face into something resembling a smile. "We're going to try joining . . ." She cleared her throat. "The Linleydale Junior Forest Rangers."

"Ta-*daaa*!" I cheered.

"You're going to *what*?" Allison shook her head as Sofía's mouth dropped open.

"Please don't take this the wrong way, baby," Sofía said. "But you hate the outdoors. Last time I suggested camping, you faked chicken pox." She ruffled Marlo's hair, tweaking one of the flyaway curls. "You're more of an indoor cat than Wade."

"I thought this was the summer of Popsicles and naps or something?" Allison set a carton of eggs on the counter and frowned at Marlo. "Why the sudden interest in Junior Forest Rangers? Seems like a bit of a left turn, honey."

"That's my fault," I piped up, eyeing Allison's skeptical gaze. "The parents are demanding I branch out this summer. I managed to convince Marlo it's worth taking our skill sets up a notch."

"*That* sounds more believable," Allison said as she set a pan out on the stove. "Not that I'm against you trying new things, Marlo. I just want to make sure you know you don't have to."

"What's not to like about it?" I asked. "Fresh air, good. Best friend, good. Sunshine—put on sunscreen—good."

Marlo rolled her eyes and smiled at her mom. "It's fine," she said as a wide grin burst across her face. "*And* Lemon's going to help me with book research for the rest of the summer, so it all evens out."

It was such a slick move I couldn't even be mad.

"All right, if this is what you want to do, we'll sign you up and buy bug spray." Allison set a bowl on the counter and grabbed the whisk. "Lemon? Fix you some eggs?"

"Any chance for pancakes?" I asked hopefully, pretty-please eyes on full blast.

"Sorry, kiddo." She smirked at me before cracking an egg over the pan. "Pancakes are for front-door users."

*M*y parents agreed to Junior Forest Rangers instantly.

They heard the words "outdoor activity" and signed the registration form in seconds.

Monday morning, Mom handed me a backpack filled with sunscreen, granola bars, a first aid kit, and rubber gloves, of all things. "You're going to have so much fun, sweetheart."

Dad patted me on the head. "I'm proud of you," he said. "I know you weren't keen on trying something new, but I think it'll be a good experience."

Oof.

A small kernel of guilt sprouted deep in my heart, and I squashed it right then and there. I might not be obeying the spirit of their directive, but if pressed, all they'd said was to "sign up" for an activity this summer. Not "and participate in every single minute of the schedule."

My parents headed out to work, and I did a once-over before setting off. I had on my new bright blue, very sturdy, slightly-too-big sneakers that Mom bought because "they'll last longer," plus Grandpa's old green fishing cap and the backpack of plenty. I was *ready*.

I trekked next door where Marlo was . . . awake-ish? She sat on her front steps, nose buried in a travel mug. Her hair was bundled in a high bun and she had ginormous sunglasses on. She barely stirred as I came up the walk.

"Is that coffee?" I asked, poking at her feet with the toe of my shoe.

"No," Marlo said mournfully. "Mom made me pour it out, but I thought sniffing the last fumes might help me wake up." She blinked at me. "It's not."

"Ooooookay." I pried the mug out of her grasp and set it on the stoop. "Upsy-daisy, my little sleepyhead. Let's get the blood flowing, and you'll be awake in no time." Offering her my hands, I hauled her to her feet.

Marlo groaned as she leaned on me. "I hate everything about this situation."

"I brought you an apple," I said, pulling the fruit out of my bag.

"Nhrgh." She batted away my offering. "Too early for that much chewing."

Prepared for that possibility, I stuffed the apple into my mouth and handed her a yogurt drink instead.

"S'better." She grabbed it, taking a swig as we headed down the walkway.

"It's seriously not going to be that bad," I said, hopping over cracks as we went. "We'll show up, get our attendance taken, hug a few trees, and then skedaddle off to start our search."

"*Skedaddle?*" Marlo stretched the word out. "You don't think someone'll notice that?"

"We'll be super stealthy," I said. "Everything's going to work perfectly. I can feel it in my bones."

"You're gonna jinx us." She rapped her knuckles on a wooden fence as we walked by.

I scoffed at the idea. We had fuel, a plan, and most importantly, optimism and enthusiasm. I sneaked a peek at Marlo's still-half-asleep face. Well, I had more than enough optimism and enthusiasm for the two of us.

No jinxing this dream team.

"We've got this," I said. "Project Validation—full speed ahead! Let me see that energy!" She rolled her eyes and I cackled as we took a sharp left, straight into Linleydale Park. Go time.

Our instructions were to meet by the pavilion, and sure enough, a group of twelve or so kids were already gathered there. Most of them were running around and goofing off as a few parents stood to the side, chatting until the leader arrived. Marlo and I kept out of the fray. None of these kids talked to me during the school year, and I sincerely hoped none of them felt the need to start now. Couldn't have them muddling the mission.

Except . . . I spotted a lone figure sitting at one of the weathered picnic tables, thoroughly engrossed in a book.

Rachel Morris. Smartest kid at our school.

Her curly black hair was pulled back in a puff, and bright purple-framed glasses perched on the end of her nose. Despite the book, she was dressed head to toe in ready-to-hike-in-the-woods gear.

I turned to my best friend. "I've had a thought."

"No." She sipped at her drink, avoiding eye contact.

"Okay, but listen," I said. "The parents want us to make new friends, right?" Pointing at Rachel, I grinned. "Rachel loves science. Aliens are science-y. Let's go talk to her."

"No." Marlo grabbed the back of my shirt. "She barely knows us. We're not going to drag her into your mission."

"I wouldn't *drag—*"

Hweet. HweetHweetHweet. HweeeEeEeeEEEt.

The rest of my argument was cut off by a short woman marching up to our group. She carried a plastic clipboard and wore a green Junior Forest Rangers cap over her brown hair. The ensemble was completed by the shiny metal whistle she was making full use of.

"Huddle up, crew!" Her voice carried across the clearing, demanding attention.

"We get through introductions and make for the woods," I whispered to Marlo as we joined the huddle. "Time to get this show on the road." The park merged into the forest, which suited my super-secret-mission purposes quite well.

"If she makes me hunt down animals, I'm out," Marlo muttered.

"It's *junior*," I said. "Junior Forest Rangers. Nothing hardcore, more like an introduction. We learn about trees and stuff."

"Welcome to the Junior Forest Rangers," the woman said. "My name is Quinn Franklin, and I'm the new leader of this program. Sound off when I call your name."

Quinn went briskly through the list, then slapped the clipboard against her leg and scrutinized our group. "If movies and television have taught us anything," she said, "it's that camping in the woods is an excellent way to die."

What.

Marlo shot me a panicked look, and I shrugged. I could respect a rousing opening speech.

"Throughout this week," Quinn continued, "if you keep your ears open and your mind sharp, I will teach you how to avoid that fate."

"I don't know what's happening," I whispered to Marlo. "But it's amazing."

Marlo shushed me, and I looked over to see her scribbling notes on a piece of paper. When did she get paper? Her hand shot up in the air, waving frantically.

Quinn nodded. "Yes, Marlo."

"Hello, hi," Marlo said. "How soon, exactly, do we learn how to not die in the woods? Is it before we enter?"

"All I'm saying is," Marlo said as we trudged through the woods, "it should be lesson number one. In class. A controlled environment. Here's what you need to know."

"Except that being in the woods is actually where we want to be," I pointed out. "Getting thrown right into it fits our game plan. Plus, *adventure!*"

Marlo hummed at me as she scanned the booklet with our first assignment—a handy plant-identifying exercise called "You Think It's Edible, but It's NOT."

I giggled as I waved my own papers at her. "It's a plant-based DIE-et. Get it? Die. Diet. Are you listening?"

Another hum was all I got as she pulled a pencil out of her pocket and started filling things in.

"Hey." I nudged her booklet. "We've got bigger things on our plate here."

Marlo stared over the top of her sunglasses. "The quickest way to get caught is to stand out. We need to know what we're supposed to be doing before we can fake it."

Oh. Right. "Attention to detail," I said, bumping hips with her. "This is why you're on the team. That, and best friendship. Look! Snacks!" I tossed her a granola bar from my bag and took one for myself.

Marlo pocketed the granola bar, returning to the booklet. "This is just"—she flipped through the pages—"a lot of ways to get a rash."

"Oooh," I said around a mouthful of bar. "That sounds interesting." I shook my head. "No. Can't get distracted. Let's split the pages and fill it out on the way."

"Compare and share at the end?" Marlo nodded. "Works for me."

Time to get down to the real stuff.

Pulling my phone out of my bag, I brought up the GPS app. "We need to go . . . that way." I pointed to the left.

Marlo took a deep breath and squared her shoulders. "Into the woods."

There were a few rough paths winding through the forest, but you could forge one if you felt bold enough. And today we were full up on bold.

Most of the JFR group wandered off in the opposite direction so the odds of anyone catching up to us were slim. Aside from the occasional bird call, the forest was quiet. We'd hear anybody roaming our way.

Traveling through the hushed space gave me plenty of time to think, and my brain said challenge accepted. All of my worries reared up to fill the silence.

Leaving the clearing on Saturday night seemed like the right thing to do at the time, but what if the aliens were already gone? I'd spent Sunday talking to Marlo and then my parents wouldn't let me leave their sight and *then* it made sense to wait until I had the rangers for cover, but now it seemed like a waste of precious time. It was a what-if avalanche, and my legs couldn't move fast enough.

We should be running to the landing site, but . . . easier said than done. I kicked at a bush in frustration. There was entirely too much shrubbery to maneuver through.

Another thought struck me.

What if we arrive and they're *still there*? I had Marlo as

backup now, but it wasn't like either of us knew what to say. What if there's special diplomatic etiquette involved? And what if I botched it? Should I have contacted the mayor's office? Or the *United Nations*?

My palms were sweaty. So gross. And unhelpful. I wiped them on my pants and glanced up, breath catching in my throat.

The clearing was just ahead.

"I don't know what you're thinking," Marlo said, poking the side of my head with her pencil. "But you look like you're about to puke, so aim that way, please. But also, I'm here, at a reasonable distance, if you need to talk."

"It's just . . ." I did a general hand flap of emotion. "It's right there. Big moment, you know?"

"The biggest."

Marlo let me have my moment . . . for a moment.

"We going in, or was this good enough for today?"

I shook out my hands and straightened up. Get it together, Lemon. "We're going in," I said. "Carefully and quietly."

Keeping to the trees for cover, we made our way over to get a better look.

A better look at the totally empty clearing.

"They were here," I said to Marlo as I stomped the rest of the way in. "I'm not lying, I swear. The ship was over there, and there was a ramp and aliens. All of it. Here."

"I believe you." Marlo turned around slowly, examining the space. "Are you sure it was *this* spot, though? Let's look at your pictures. Check the landmarks. Or maybe their technology messed with your phone? Or maybe—"

"Or maybe they're gone and we missed them." I flopped down on the grass. "This was my chance! My one chance, and I messed it up!"

She dropped beside me. "Does this mean we can quit Junior Forest Rangers?"

"You're not funny!"

"Sorry, bad joke," Marlo said, pulling my hands away from my face. "We need to regroup. Let's stay here for a minute and figure out a new plan." She lay down, settling her bag as a pillow. "Mama always says meditation can help you work through a problem."

Meditation. I didn't know how lying here and breathing and communing with the universe was going to bring the aliens back. Unless I could commune my way into their Wi-Fi.

"Do you hear that?" Marlo whispered.

"What?"

"Stop thinking so loud and listen," she hissed.

I zipped my lips and closed my eyes, prepared to open up my ears.

First . . . the soft rustle of wind through the trees.

Gentle bird calls and tiny scratching sounds from bugs on the ground.

Far-off shouts from the JFR kids.

And . . . something . . . underneath it all. A little buzz, out of tune with everything else.

My eyes snapped open and I looked over to see Marlo watching me carefully.

"There you go," she said. "Weird, right?"

"What do you think it is?"

Marlo chewed her lip in thought. "It sounds electric. No power lines around here though. What else would use that much energy?"

"Whoa." I sat up to peer around the clearing. "Do you think they're cloaking their ship?"

"It's not any weirder than the rest of it."

"That—that might be worse!" My little flicker of hope fizzled out in an instant. "How are we supposed to find them if we can't even *see* them?"

"What are you doing?" Rachel stepped out from the trees to cast a suspicious eye over us sprawled on the ground.

"Rachel, hi!" I scrambled up, dusting the dirt off my legs. "We were taking a break and working on a little problem. Would you happen to know anything about camouflaging systems?"

Marlo shushed me, pulling at my jeans, and I waved her off.

Rachel adjusted her glasses, considering the question. "What's that have to do with our assignment?" She pulled the day's pamphlet out of her back pocket.

"Absolutely nothing." Marlo tilted her head to look up at her. "It's for a puzzle from Lemon's grandpa."

I scowled at Marlo for lying, but she was unbothered.

"If it helps," Rachel said. "My mom always says the simplest answer is usually the right one. Good luck." She walked off, and I crouched down next to Marlo.

"Why did you do that? It was the perfect opening!" We could've briefed her on Project Validation and had the benefit of three brains working on our little pickle.

"Not everyone is prepared for your brand of shenanigans," Marlo said, continuing on before I could list the many ways I took offense to that statement. "Do you want to spend the rest of the day trying to convince her that aliens are real, *or* let her go so we can dive back into the problem at hand?"

"You don't know she would have needed convincing," I grumbled. "She was already offering help and she didn't even know what the problem was!"

Rachel's suggestion of the simplest answer looped around my brain. What could be—

Oh.

OH.

"Marlo!"

"Right beside you, buddy."

I batted excitedly at her shoulder. "Okay, so the aliens have superior technology to hide their ship from our sight, and we don't have the tech to combat that."

"Accurate."

"But we don't have to be at their level to find them," I said. "Not if we go for the simplest solution."

"Explain, please?" Marlo asked. "Because I'm not following."

"Behind their cloaking tech is still a ship," I said. "Made of *metal*. Let's go see a man about a metal detector."

Marlo sat up. "You think that'll work?"

"Only one way to find out," I said.

Gnedley

"Ensign. Ensign Gnedley."

Gnedley groaned and cracked one eye open to see Doctor Gnog and Chief Gneelix looming over him. "Gah!" He flailed, tangling his limbs in the blanket, nearly tumbling to the ground in the process. "Uh." Gnedley tried to gather his words as his pulse pounded in his ears.

"A splendid morning to you, Ensign," Doctor Gnog grinned.

Gneelix kicked a sturdy black boot against his bunk. "Hurry up if you want to eat breakfast while it's freshly rehydrated," she said.

"It's blue today," Doctor Gnog added. "Such fun."

Gnedley was beginning to suspect prolonged periods of living on a ship had altered their perception of "fun."

After the wake-up call that set his hearts pumping, Gnog and Gneelix left him to get ready for the day. Putting on his uniform helped calm Gnedley. They might be stranded on an alien planet, but his uniform remained unchanged.

Black pants, red tunic.

Black boots, red cap.

Utility belt around his waist, communicator on his wrist, and logbook in hand.

Properly equipped, Gnedley stalked out of the room. His rehydrated breakfast wasn't going to eat itself.

Yesterday, Captain Gnemo had declared they'd make the best of their situation while Gneelix repaired the ship, so Gnemo, Gnilsson, and Gnog went to gather samples. Gnedley was left behind to refresh his knowledge of the Isolated Community standard protocol and emergency measures handbook and learn it word for word. The captain was taking no chances.

Perhaps *today* he'd get to venture beyond the shields.

Gneelix shoved a plate of blue sludge into his hands when Gnedley arrived at the mess area they'd set up outside the loading bay doors. Gnog had prescribed fresh air and sunshine to combat the stress of their circumstances. Given the increasing rants from Gneelix as she contended with the ship's repairs, Gnedley wasn't sure it was working.

"I refitted that seal before we launched," Gneelix snapped at Gnog as she plopped down on a crate. "Makes zero sense for it to leak already."

"I'm sure it's not your fault," the doctor replied mildly.

"My fau—of course not!" Gneelix sputtered. "I'm the reason we manage to fly more than two feet off the ground in the first place. Which is why I know—"

"You'll have us ready to go in no time," Doctor Gnog agreed. "I should collect my samples while I can. You'll be all right on your own, Ensign?"

Not leaving the ship after all then. Gnedley nodded as he gulped down the remaining dregs of his truly disgusting meal.

The doctor gathered their supplies, tottering off through the barrier with a wave.

"Don't break anything, don't go beyond the shield, and don't bother me." Gneelix stabbed a finger at him and snarled. "Got it?"

"Yes, Chief Gneelix," Gnedley said, adding a smart salute for good measure.

She grunted and spun off to continue her battle with the repairs.

"Good chat," Gnedley muttered to himself.

Clearing away his dishes, he pulled out his logbook and set to work registering the last of yesterday's samples. He picked up a sealed and labeled canister. Along the side was the

Gnomish title, as well as the Human classification.

Pine needles.

Gnedley rolled the strange words around in his mouth and shook the container, watching the tiny green sticks clink against the sides. Fascinating.

So absorbed in his work, Gnedley barely noticed the hours tick by. He looked up at the sound of someone entering the clearing, expecting to see the captain or Gnilsson returning from their rounds. Instead, it was merely two Humans. Juveniles, at first inspection. Maybe the cap—

Gnedley whipped back around to the barrier, jaw dropping in shock.

Humans.

Beside their ship.

Great Gnominium.

He could hear the buzz of their voices, but it was too far away for his translator to decipher any conversation. Gnedley paused. The shield projected a low-level pulse to deter creatures, and no IC tech could detect it. Surely it would be safe enough. . . .

There was no resisting the pull to get a closer look.

Especially since there were three of them now!

What were they speaking of? What were they doing out in these woods?

Gnedley was suddenly hit by the downside of their protocols. He knew the rules kept crews and IC residents safe, but in this moment? What would it be like to step through the barrier and introduce himself? Seize the opportunity and learn about 525-1 directly from Humans?

Question after question was building up inside him. What did snow taste like? What was it like to have a . . . what was their name for it? A *feline*.

Did they ever wonder about the worlds beyond their own?

What questions did *they* have?

The temptation to speak with the Humans was strong, but . . . he sighed as he watched them leave. Someday 525-1 would no longer be an IC planet, and he would be able to speak to *every* resident. Until then, they had plenty of other methods to gather knowledge for the Alliance. He picked up another sample and got back to work.

As 525-1's sun began to set, Captain Gnemo and Doctor Gnog returned.

"This looks thoroughly organized, Gnedley," Captain Gnemo said, surveying his work. "Hopefully Gneelix has made as much progress with the *Gnar Five*."

"I wouldn't bring that up if I were you, Captain," Gnedley whispered.

Gneelix's mood hadn't improved as she delved further into the heart of the ship, and Gnedley had learned a number of shocking new phrases during the day.

"Captain, you should see this." Commander Gnilsson had emerged through the shield, a small figure in his arms.

Captain Gnemo stiffened at the sight, and Gnedley leaned forward to get a better look.

It was a miniature gnome.

That on its own was unremarkable. Gnedley remembered his Alliance history well. The early years were fraught with missteps on IC planets, and it was an age before proper protocols were consistently enforced. Imprints of those initial visits remained.

But the last recorded exposure on 525-1 had been centuries ago. And for this level of accuracy, the local inhabitants must have had a recent encounter with an Alliance gnome. An ensign, judging by the red uniform. One who had failed disastrously at following protocol.

"Captain?" Gnilsson's voice startled Gnedley out of his thoughts. The first officer was waving the statue at Gnemo, who stood frozen in place.

"What should I do with this?" he asked.

The captain gave herself a small shake and cleared her throat. "It's not our place to remove artifacts, Commander Gnilsson."

"A rustic likeness is one thing, Captain," he said, side-eyeing the statue. "Should we really be leaving this on an IC planet and risking further spread?"

Gnedley attempted to appear busy while tension rose in the clearing. The statue had put the whole crew on edge, but Captain Gnemo seemed particularly strained.

"Secure it for now," she said sharply. "I'll consult with HQ when comms are back."

Gnilsson saluted with the statue and strode up the ramp into the hold.

Gnemo muttered softly to herself before noticing the three sets of eyes still on her. "Gneelix," she snapped. "How long until comms are up and running?"

"I've been a little focused on the holes—" Gneelix said, her face scrunching up.

"Make it soon." Gnemo stomped off into the ship.

Gneelix ripped off her hat and squeezed it in one fist. "I am *one* gnome."

"I'll start dinner." Doctor Gnog patted her shoulder. "We'll have the red stuff."

Gneelix tilted her head and considered that. "I don't hate the red stuff."

"I know," Gnog smiled.

"Ensign, quit gawking and help Doc with dinner." Gneelix grunted, hefting her tool bag.

"Aye, Chief." Gnedley hopped to it, mind spinning with what he'd witnessed. He thought he'd been well prepared before joining this mission, but clearly there was more to the Alliance's history with 525-1 than Gnedley realized.

What other secrets were hiding here?

CHAPTER 7

Secrets were the worst.

I loved *fun* ones—like hiding Marlo's birthday present, but then caving and telling her because it was too exciting not to. Lucky for me she never got mad.

But *important* secrets that you couldn't decide if you should keep or not because you couldn't figure out what was the right thing to do and it was driving you nuts....

Those were the worst.

I didn't tell Grandpa why we needed the metal detector when we'd picked it up from him yesterday afternoon. I told him we had a lead, but not about Saturday night. I didn't want to get his hopes up! These aliens might not be from the same galaxy as Gnemo, much less the same planet. I fingers-crossed hoped they were, but the odds—well, I was optimistically ignoring the odds.

Which left me coming down the stairs on Tuesday morning with a backpack full of metal detector and half-truths. I jiggled the bag. Probably room for granola bars still.

Detouring into the kitchen, I stopped in my tracks at the sight of Dad flipping pancakes at the stove and Mom sipping her tea, scrolling through the morning news.

"Hi, honey!" She smiled at my sudden appearance. "Family breakfast!"

I gently lowered my bag to the floor, hoping nothing clinked loudly enough to attract attention. "Why aren't you at work?"

"Since there wasn't time to celebrate your *first* day of camp . . ." She patted the chair beside her. "We're giving you a second-day send-off!"

Dad slid a plate piled high with pancakes onto the table, taking a seat on my other side. "You can tell us what's planned for the rest of the week."

Breakfast with a side of parental interrogation. "Gosh," I said. "That sounds great."

Okay. Don't panic. A little selective storytelling *and* you get pancakes out of the deal.

"It's been fun," I said, stuffing a bite into my mouth. Parents ask way less questions if you distract them with disgusting table manners. "We yerned all inds a uff ye'erday."

"That's great," Mom said. "Now swallow and tell us about it properly."

Foiled. I chugged some juice and regrouped. "No, yeah, it's awesome," I said. "We learned about what plants are edible and what's not. I could totally make a danger salad now."

"Neat." Dad exchanged a look with Mom. "Who's teaching this again?"

"Quinn Franklin? Marlo's convinced she wasn't actually hired," I said. "Just emerged from the forest to teach us her ways."

"Sounds like useful stuff." Mom rested her chin in her hand. "What's today's topic?"

I shrugged. "Quinn says the element of surprise is part of our survivalist training."

Dad snorted into his coffee. "Takes me back to my scout days."

"And Marlo's enjoying herself?" Mom asked.

"You know Marlo," I said. "She's getting good story ideas out of it. There's a campground murder mystery brewing."

"I used to go camping with my parents," Dad said. "I remember lying under the stars and Walt pointing out constellations."

"He did? Which one's your favorite? Mine's—"

"Pegasus," Dad and I said at the same time.

"Really?" That surprised me. "Grandpa told me the planets there were the first ones telescopes on Earth could see beyond our own solar system. Is that why you liked it?"

"More because flying horse." Dad laughed. "Didn't exactly think about it scientifically."

"Okay, but it *is* actually so cool," I said, pushing my plate away. "It's far, but not as *space* far as other things, so kind of close when you think about it. Maybe Grandpa's alien is—"

Dad rose to rinse his plate in the sink before leaning up against the counter. "Pretty sure it's easier to picture it as a cool flying horse."

And that was why Project Validation existed. To show Dad that all that space out there is full of *life*, not just stars and planets. Maybe even an actual flying horse or two.

"We should talk to Sofía and Allison," Mom said brightly, breaking the silence. "Set up a camping adventure before summer's over."

Marlo would one hundred percent kill me if I helped set up more outdoor activities. "Let's see if we survive Junior Forest Rangers first."

"I've got a lot of projects on the go," Dad said as he grabbed the rest of the breakfast plates, avoiding eye contact. "I might have to miss out."

"Before I forget . . ." Mom slapped a hand down on the table. "Mrs. Harrison on the corner asked if we'd seen her new garden gnome. It went missing last night."

"Not me, I swear," I said. "I've got better things to do with my time than steal people's garden gnomes." Like look for the real thing.

"What about you, sweetheart?" She grinned over at Dad, who scowled. What?

"No," he said.

"Are you sure? She asked about you specifically." Mom hid a snort behind her mug, and I was definitely missing something.

"Why would she ask about *Dad*?"

"Nobody's seen it," Dad said tersely, spine rigid. "End of discussion."

"Honey." Mom got up to give him a squeeze. "Can't we laugh about it a little now?"

"Laugh about *what*?" I spun around in my seat, exasperated.

Dad groaned, closing his eyes while Mom patted his chest. "When he was a teenager, your dad had a minor reputation for being a garden gnome thief."

My jaw dropped. "You're joking." For someone who hated the whole garden gnome thing, that seemed pretty involved.

"Nope," Mom said. "The whole town was up in arms about it. People hosted stakeouts to catch him in the act."

I couldn't believe it. The man went on a full-on crime spree, and I'd been kept in the dark about it for almost *twelve whole years*. "How did you get caught?"

"I didn't." Dad grabbed the syrup and tossed it back in the fridge. "Figured out it wasn't accomplishing what I wanted, so I returned what I had. Paid for the damaged ones. Not an exciting story."

"Says you. How many did you steal? And you *broke* some? *Why?*"

"I thought . . . out of sight, out of mind." He grimaced. "I wanted to go *one week* without people harassing me about little green space gnomes, but it only added fuel to the fire."

"People are dumb, Dad." Plenty of kids teased me about the alien thing, but what did I care? I had Marlo and Grandpa. "You have to ignore them."

"Took me a lot longer than you to learn that lesson, kiddo," Dad said. "And obviously some people in this town never forget." He glanced at the clock on the microwave. "Gotta run. Tell Mrs. Harrison her gnome is safe from me. She can point her bony finger elsewhere."

"I will definitely paraphrase that." Mom kissed his cheek as he grabbed his keys and left.

Hunh. My whole worldview had suddenly tilted sideways. I tried to picture teen Dad skulking around, swiping garden gnomes, but any way I shaped it, it refused to make sense. "He literally stole garden gnomes from people's actual yards?"

"Your dad doesn't like to talk about the past a lot." Mom sat back down after delivering the understatement of the century. "It's different for you," she continued. "Enough time has passed that it's more history than news. But when it first happened, people were relentless." She sighed softly. "Your dad was teased for *years*. I think stealing the gnomes was him trying to take control of the situation."

"Did you know him back then? Partners in crime?"

"No." She laughed. "We met after high school, but he told me all about it once. Wanted me to know what I was marrying into."

"And you still said yes."

"Of course I did." She tweaked my nose. "Turned out pretty okay too. Now scoot! If you're late, Marlo might go back to bed."

I snuck a look at the time and yikes, she was right. "Love you, bye," I said, grabbing my bag and booking it for the door.

"Keep an eye out for that gnome," she called after me.

Planning on it.

* * *

Despite the family breakfast delay, Marlo and I made it to Junior Forest Rangers bright and early, ready to level up our search. Today was the day. I could *feel it*.

Quinn side-eyed me as she gathered everyone, and Marlo elbowed my ribs. "Quit vibrating," she muttered. "You look suspicious."

"Can I help it if I'm filled with excitement?" I whispered. "Full of hope at the possibility of my dreams coming true. Ready to face the day, meet its challenges, and emerge triumphant."

"Ready to get caught if you don't shu—uh, say thank you to Quinn for today's assignment," Marlo redirected loudly as she accepted our handouts.

"Look alive out there, kids," Quinn growled before striding off to distribute what was probably a thrilling, yet terrifying, read to the rest of the group.

"Looking alive, looking sharp, looking for aliens." I shimmied at Marlo, unable to stay still if I tried. I had it—that feeling when a plan's coming together. When you're so pumped up, you feel like you can do anything, but also like you might puke a bit. The *best* feeling.

Once again, we steadily made our exit, trudging beyond the paths until we were back at yesterday's spot. I pulled Grandpa's metal detector out of my bag and started putting it together.

Eye on the prize. Focused on the task at hand.

"So, geese are the worst," Marlo said, skimming through today's booklet, titled "Things That Bite, Things That Sting, Things That Beat You with Their Wings."

"How so?" I grunted as I screwed the handle into the top end of the pole.

"They will take you *down*. No regrets."

"Really." I flipped the switch on the metal detector, pleased when the screen came to life.

"Wouldn't that be a great murder-mystery twist?" Marlo pulled a notebook out of her bag and started scribbling. "The culprit's a goose, but it gets away because everyone's too afraid to go and arrest it." She snickered to herself as she finished her notes.

That snicker was suspicious. "Do *not* name someone Lemon so you can kill me off with a goose, Marlo!"

She wrote faster.

"Why would a goose murder someone, though?"

Marlo shot me a flat look. "You didn't read the booklet."

"I've been on task." I swung the metal detector in front of her. "Look at this beauty!"

"It looks very detector-y," Marlo said graciously.

Exactly what we needed to get the job done. "Let's go find a spaceship!"

* * *

"Useless piece of junk," I grumbled, and flopped against a tree. The change in my pocket jingled, making me even more annoyed. All we had to show after an hour of scanning was a grubby dollar and sixty-five cents. "I really thought this would work."

The simple piece of technology they hadn't accounted for. The crack in their shields. The undiscovered flaw in their defenses. Their only weakness—

"Maybe their ship isn't metal," Marlo said.

Wha—?

Hmm.

Bit annoyed we didn't think of that before spending an hour sweating and chasing after beeps. With no next moves jumping out of the ol' brain cells, I was well and truly stumped. "What are we missing?" I asked. "We've searched the whole clearing. Using *multiple* methods."

"No, you haven't."

We jumped as Rachel popped out from behind the tree.

"Yes, we have," I said, whisking the metal detector out of her reach before she could finish poking at it. "I think I know how to walk in a circle."

Rachel arched a brow at me. "Do you, though?" She stepped to the edge of the clearing. "I've been watching. You walk halfway and then turn around. Ever heard of a grid pattern?"

I scoffed. "We searched everywhere. Right, Marlo?"

"I thought we did." She shrugged. "But if Rachel saw us turn around . . ."

Well, now it was going to bug me.

"Here's the plan." I nudged at Marlo until she stood beside Rachel. "I'm going to walk all the way around the clearing, and you'll watch me do it. Okay?"

I switched the metal detector back on, because if I was doing this, I might as well do a fifth sweep while I was at it. Eyes sharp and ears tuned in, I marched around the clearing.

Nothing over here.

Nothing over here.

Nothing over here.

I stomped back to Marlo and Rachel. "See? Nothing."

Rachel cleared her throat and Marlo looked stunned. Not exactly the reaction I was looking for. "What?"

"You took a left turn about halfway and missed the whole back section," Marlo said.

"*What?*" That was just bananas. I spun around to look. "No way."

"Told you." Rachel crossed her arms with a smirk.

"Let's get to the bottom of this." Herding Marlo and Rachel along, I dashed back to the edge of the clearing. "Together.

Slowly," I said. "Wait until we think we're at the end."

The three of us crept forward, arms waving, probably looking like fools, but I didn't sign up for this mission to look cool. Soon we were at the wall of trees.

"Strange," Rachel said. "It does seem like we've walked to the end, but when I watched from a distance, you never made it this far. And it *feels* like we should turn."

"An optical illusion?" Marlo eyed the trees, arms crossed. "That causes misdirection?"

"One way to find out." I lifted the metal detector.

"No!" Marlo tried to knock it out of my hand, but nothing was stopping me. I waved it in front of us until it looked like it was going *into* the trees, and there was a sharp crackling noise.

The air in front of us *rippled* in rolling waves that spread out, disappearing into the sky.

Interesting. I hit it a few more times. *Bzzt. Bzzzt. Bzzzzt.* The crackling noise was so familiar. Like bugs hitting a zapper!

Were we the bugs in this case?

"Some kind of shield?" Rachel stepped closer, reaching out to touch whatever it was, but Marlo was quicker this time.

"Not with your hands!" She pulled Rachel back and got in front of me at the same time. "That's not a friendly 'Welcome!' sound. We shouldn't touch it when we don't know what it is."

"Ooh!" Thank goodness for overpacking moms. "Rubber

gloves! One sec." I dug through my backpack until I found the heavy plastic gloves Mom had thrown in there. "Who knew these would come in handy?"

"Bad idea," Marlo said. "That force field or whatever could cause actual damage."

I snapped the gloves on. "I'll be gentle."

"You're seriously . . . I can't watch." Marlo buried her face in her hands while Rachel stepped closer.

"I can," she said. "For science."

For science. For aliens. For Grandpa Walt.

"Here it goes." I took a deep breath and stretched out my left arm. Taking one step forward, I extended my pointer finger . . . and poked.

Bzzzzzzzt.

"Did she die?" Marlo cried.

"I'm fine!" I said, watching the ripples flutter out from where I'd touched. It actually made some pretty patterns in the air. I poked a few more times for good measure.

Bzzt. Bzzzzt. Bzzzzzzzt. Bzt. Bzt. Bzzzzt.

Marlo slapped my arm. "Would you please stop before something blows up?"

"It's not doing anything though," I said. "Look. It bounces right back. I think it really is some type of cloaking force field."

Rachel made grabby hands at the gloves. "I want to try."

"Knock yourself out," I said, peeling them off.

"Not literally," Marlo pleaded.

Fearless in the name of science, Rachel reached out with both gloved hands and *pushed*.

BZZZZZZZZZZZZZZT.

That sounded angrier. Maybe it could only handle so much before shorting out. "Let's try it together," I said to Rachel.

She passed me a glove and we traveled back and forth, poking and prodding while Marlo moaned the whole time. We didn't bust through, but—

"I'm not imagining this, right?" I said to Marlo. "This is definitely *something*."

"Yeah." She let out a little amazed laugh. "I think it is."

Grandpa and I never found any real evidence during our searches, so this? This was big. And now we had someone who could help unlock the rest of the puzzle.

I looked at Rachel, who stared back, biting her lip. She nodded to herself. Like she'd made up her mind about something.

"There's something else you should see."

CHAPTER 8

Rachel bustled us through the woods. "I wasn't sure if it was a mutation," she said, excitement speeding up her voice. "Or something more unusual." She stopped to crouch in front of a cluster of stumps set in a loose circle. "Look."

You know that moment before you go down a slide and your stomach does a little dance because everything's about to *whoosh*? Whatever this was, wherever it was going to lead, I knew it was going to whoosh big-time.

We stepped over to see what Rachel was gazing at so reverently.

"Mushrooms?" Would not have even made my top fifty guesses.

"Oooh, are those jack-o'-lantern mushrooms?" Marlo sat

on a stump to peer at the clumps growing through the center of the ring.

"*Omphalotus illudens*?" Rachel asked.

"Sure," Marlo said, waving a hand through the air. "They glow in the dark and they're poisonous, right? Pretty sure they were on the do-not-eat list."

"Very." Rachel nodded. "But I don't think that's what these are. The convex cap and sharp gills are correct, but the color is on the golden side, while the spore print is green toned. *And* it's much too early for them to be growing in this area."

"You know a lot about mushrooms," I said, impressed. "Like, you used 'spore print' in a sentence." I wasn't entirely sure what that *was*, but it sounded like Intense Science Knowledge.

Rachel smiled shyly. "I'm an amateur mycologist."

"Amazing! What's that?"

"I study mushrooms," she said. "Their properties and uses. Did you know some mushrooms can break down plastics?"

"Really?" Marlo perked up, fingers already pulling her notebook out of her bag. "What about a dead body?"

Rachel nodded hesitantly. "There are companies developing ways to use them for greener burials."

"Less evidence," Marlo muttered to herself.

"*What?*"

"Ignore her," I stepped in. "She's book plotting. Not evil plotting."

That didn't seem to provide as much comfort as it was meant to. "You love mushrooms!" I redirected. "That's cool. I didn't know about the plastic thing."

Rachel's enthusiasm grew, her glasses slipping down her nose as she nodded. "Fungi are the future! We have an amazing variety of species growing in our woods. My ultimate goal this summer is to try and hybridize one that's hearty enough to grow in a variety of environments while capitalizing on its decomposition capabilities."

"Wow!" I only understood half of that, but if there's one thing I could get, it was working toward a goal with single-minded focus. The most quality of qualities.

"That was probably more information than you wanted." Rachel trailed off with a wince. "Sorry, people usually stop me by now."

"Why? It's interesting."

She squinted at me. "Are you being sarcastic?"

"Nope," Marlo piped up from her notes. "When Lemon's sarcastic she uses jazz hands."

"Helpful commentary, *Marlo*—" I caught her smirk and looked down at my waggling fingers. "Any. Way." I focused on Rachel. "Back to the weird mushrooms that don't look right and shouldn't be growing here."

"That's the weirder part!" Rachel exclaimed. "I'm in these woods every weekend. My mom's a botanist so she likes to show me things in the field. We were here on Sunday, and those mushrooms *weren't*."

"Isn't growth, like, number-one plant goals?" I asked.

"It's abnormal," Rachel said. "There's no way they would have matured this much."

"Maybe it's really good soil?" Marlo suggested.

"Even that wouldn't explain the *weirdest* part." She looked at Marlo and me. Waiting.

"What's the weirdest part, Rachel?" I asked.

Leaning toward the closest mushroom, she tapped it with one finger. It instantly lit up, casting a soft golden glow across her warm brown skin.

That was definitely the weirdest part.

"*Omphalotus illudens* is capable of bioluminescence, but it's a faint green-blue color," she explained. "And no known species of fungi illuminates on demand. And that's not all."

My mind spun with information overload. I didn't know how much more I could take in.

Who was I kidding? This was amazing. "What else?"

"Look at this." Rachel pointed to some metal triangles I'd missed, sticking out in a few odd spots around the mushrooms.

Marlo peered at them over my shoulder.

"I've been searching online," Rachel said, brushing dirt away from one of the triangles. "But I can't find this symbol or these letters in any records." She pointed to an etching in the metal. It looked like a leaf with a design in the center. I didn't recognize it either.

This was definitely worth the field trip. "So you think," I said slowly, carefully, because it felt like too much to hope for. "The mushrooms and the metal might be connected to our invisible wall?"

"It's my latest hypothesis," she said.

I poked one of the mushrooms, watching it light up. "Do you believe in fate?"

Marlo groaned as Rachel scrunched her nose at me.

"Scientifically speaking?" She shook her head. "Coincidence isn't grounds for evidence."

"I'm thinking we were *meant* to run into each other at Junior Forest Rangers," I said.

"Statistically, if you factor in the population with the number of activities available—"

"And I think we're meant to *help* each other." The stars aligned to assist with our search for life among them.

"Lemon." Marlo's voice held a clear note of warning.

"What?" Who was I to argue with fate? "She likes science. If our two science things are related, shouldn't we work together?"

"You can say no," Marlo assured Rachel. "And we should probably fill you in on the whole alien-search thing first."

"Why are you making that sound like an apology?" We were letting her in on the opportunity of a lifetime!

"I pretty much know already." Rachel shrugged. "Everyone's heard about Lemon's grandpa, and you've been talking about—what's it called? Project Validation?—pretty much nonstop since yesterday."

Hunh.

"You know what?" I clapped my hands together. "Not having to explain saves time. And lesson learned regarding our whispering skills."

"Your whispering skills," Marlo muttered.

No need to dignify that with a response. "What do you think, Rachel? Gonna help us track down some aliens?"

"It *would* be mutually beneficial to combine resources," Rachel said, pondering it. "If you help me study the mushrooms and collect more samples, I'll help with your search. Maybe answers for one will lead to answers for another."

"See?" I beamed at Marlo. "Rachel gets it! Welcome to the team. We need T-shirts."

"And if we find these aliens," Rachel continued. "It would be the scientific breakthrough of a lifetime. Proof of life on other planets? Sentient beings? *And*—" She tripped over her own words as her excitement gathered steam. "The mushrooms? Their organisms thriving on our planet? The possibilities could change the *world*."

"What if it's dangerous?" Marlo said abruptly. "I'm not trying to rain on everyone's parade here, but we're hoping this is Lemon's grandpa's alien, right? But it could be an *evil* alien who won't be happy we're messing with their crop."

Rachel and I took a step back as we looked over the patch with new perspective.

"Evil aliens who won't want to leave any witnesses," Marlo whispered.

We stared at the mushrooms, and a chill ran down my spine.

This was getting ridiculous. I shook myself to get rid of the heebie-jeebies. "I *hope* it's Grandpa's alien," I said. "But you're right—it could be someone without good intentions."

"What do we do?" Marlo asked.

"Process of elimination," Rachel said. "We work on learning about the mushrooms and the shield and the aliens in turn. Do our best to be careful, and see what we find."

"Best case scenario," I said. "It's friendly aliens and we can talk to them about sharing information. That work for you, Rachel?"

Rachel was silent as she thought it over for a few minutes. "It sounds reasonable."

Marlo raised a hand. "What's the worst-case scenario plan?"

"We run?"

Rachel nodded while Marlo squinched up her face at my suggestion.

"Bringing Rachel on board was supposed to improve our plans," she said. "Okay, fine. We run and hope we don't die. Count me in."

"Great," I cheered. "Everyone's on the same page. I think now's an excellent time to go and visit Grandpa Walt. I have *questions*."

"First things first." Rachel grabbed a couple of trowels out of her pack and tossed them at me and Marlo. "I need more soil samples."

We did agree to help with Rachel's side of the equation. Never let it be said I wasn't a good team member. "Deal. Dirt, then Walt."

"Could the mushrooms decompose bones, or just flesh?" Marlo held her notebook propped up on her knees, pen in one hand, vial of dirt in the other. She'd been picking Rachel's brain throughout the entire sample session.

I burst out laughing. "How disgusting is this book going to be?"

"I need to know all the possibilities before I pick a path," she sniffed primly.

"Rachel's not gonna want to work with us if you keep being gross," I teased.

"I don't mind." Rachel smiled. "It's nice having someone interested in all of this."

"She doesn't mind." Marlo shot me a smirk. "I'm putting Rachel on the list of characters *not* to kill off."

Rachel's grin widened when I squawked. Picking up a clump of dirt on my trowel, I flung it in Marlo's direction. She ducked smoothly out of the way.

"Respect the research site!" Rachel yelped.

Bzzzt.

Her protests cut off as we all recognized the sound. The dirt bounced off the empty air behind Marlo, creating the same ripples we'd seen in the clearing.

"What the—" I reached out with the trowel and poked, testing the resistance. "It's another wall. Do you think those metal things have something to do with it?"

"Hard to say," Rachel said. "If they help create the barrier, maybe those ones are faulty or forgotten extras. If we could find the source . . . ," she murmured to herself, walking carefully around and measuring the perimeter.

I tapped on the invisible wall, listening to it hum.

"This spot is louder," I said, realization clicking into place. "The other one made noise when we touched it, but didn't keep going like this."

The humming intensified until there was a flash, and the scene before us changed. Ten small metal plates appeared, driven into the ground in a loose circle, and in the center of it—

"It's the mother lode," Rachel whispered.

Crammed within the circle were hundreds of the strange mushrooms.

"The plot thickens," Marlo said, crouching to get a better look.

"Careful." Rachel held her back. "We don't know if the barrier's burned out or glitching. We can't risk getting caught behind it."

"Or in the middle of it." A mess too scary to imagine. I scanned the woods for any clues as to who had left this mini shield and where they might have gone.

"I'd love to take one of these home to study," Rachel said, poking at a plate wistfully with her trowel. "Take it apart and see what's inside."

"I hate to curb the march of scientific progress, but you're right," I said. "Getting too close is a bad idea. More importantly, this is another clue."

"Clues aren't more important than safety, Lemon," Marlo chided.

"Agree to disagree." I waved a hand at her.

Rachel gave the plate one final tap. She leaped back as the air crackled and the barrier snapped into place.

"Okay, that thing is freaky," Marlo shuddered.

"It could be on a timer," Rachel said. "We'll have to study it in place."

"Grab some leaves." I ran my feet over the dirt around the visible mushrooms. "We need to cover our tracks so they don't know we were here. If everything's intact, we have a better chance of catching up with them."

Marlo and Rachel helped me put things back to their natural appearance. I checked over our work, nodding in satisfaction as I dusted my hands.

"Now what?" Marlo asked.

I grinned. "Now we consult our expert."

Gnedley

The day had had such a promising start.

Immediately after breakfast, Gnilsson handed him a sample bag. "Captain says you're ready for the field as long as you stay within the coordinates I sent to your logbook."

Gnedley ran a hand reverently over the Alliance logo on the flap. He could hardly believe this moment had finally arrived. Only one thing was missing.

The commander winced at Gnedley's wandering look. "She'd be here to see you off," he explained. "But getting the comms up and running is first priority."

Gnedley could hardly argue with that.

"Good luck, and please return with all of your limbs intact," Gnilsson continued with a wink. "No one needs that paperwork." He saluted as Gnedley crossed through the barrier and strode into the woods with his head held high.

Portable shield activated, Gnedley reviewed the coordinates on his logbook and then opened a new file so he could document every step. He didn't want to forget a single second when he wrote home about his adventures.

Midday, he spotted the Humans from yesterday, tromping through the forest.

An opportunity to safely observe them interacting in their natural habitat? How could he resist? Gnedley followed, pausing when they strayed beyond the bounds the captain had limited him to. But then they spoke of aliens and shields and he kept close until—

They'd led him to *this*.

Gnedley had not survived his first crash-landing on his first alien planet during his first Alliance mission in order to have to deal with *this*.

He stared at the highly illegal crop of illicit mushrooms in dismay.

Smugglers? On an IC planet?

Except those shield plates were Alliance technology.

Could they be stolen? Pirates made no bones about using whatever they could scavenge.

Another explanation. A worse one.

They had been set up by a crew member.

Gnedley watched in silent horror as the Humans poked at the precious mushrooms that villains across the universe *killed* to get their hands on.

Did they know what was at their fingertips? Where they came from?

Were they involved in this horrible, day-ruining business somehow?

The captain. He shook himself out of his stupor, exiting without a sound. She'd know what to do. Gnedley turned to run back through the woods toward the ship. His hearts beat in double time, blood rushing through his ears a background pulse to the only thought in his brain.

Find the captain.

Muscles straining, he tripped over plants, sample vials rattling at his side. Halfway there, sweat running down his face—

Bam.

Gnedley ran smack into a tree.

"Ensign?"

Not a tree. Commander Gnilsson.

"What did you find?" he asked, eyes concerned as he held Gnedley steadily upright by the shoulders. "What's wrong?"

"I . . . I . . ."

"Slow down," he said. "Whatever it is, I can help."

Of course! Gnilsson was second-in-command. The next best thing to Gnemo. Gnedley detailed everything he'd seen, nerves rising as the commander's frown deepened.

"Show me," he bit out.

Gnedley struggled to catch up as Gnilsson dashed ahead. Before long, they were back in the clearing, and the Humans were nowhere in sight. The commander crouched to examine the mushrooms.

"You shouldn't be out here," he murmured to the small, visible cluster.

"The shields are set up right there," Gnedley pointed. "What do you think, sir? Since we can't contact HQ, should we—"

"Stop." Gnilsson sat on one of the stumps, gesturing for Gnedley to do the same. "We're in a delicate spot," he said. "It could be smugglers, but we both know there's a second option." Gnedley nodded slowly.

"I didn't want to believe it would come to this, but . . ." Gnilsson pinned Gnedley with an intense stare. "How much do you know about the captain's history?"

Aside from memorizing her career path and every scientific paper she'd penned? "Some," Gnedley said. "What does that have to do with *this*?"

"Possibly everything," Gnilsson said. "This planet, 525-1, is on our restricted list because of Gnemo. *She's* the one who's not supposed to travel here. If our communications were functional, a relief ship would arrive to ensure we weren't on planet a moment longer than necessary."

That didn't make any sense. "But—"

"Remember the statue I found?" Gnilsson's shoulders hunched forward, like he was weighed down by the story he was about to reveal, and suddenly Gnedley didn't want to hear it.

He didn't want to share that weight.

"It was Gnemo," Gnilsson said. "During her last mission here, she met with a Human and broke protocol, revealing classified information. She should have been discharged. But somehow it got buried."

Gnedley's head spun. *Their* captain, who was to lead them, keep them safe, and uphold the ideals of the Alliance, had broken the golden rule. Gnedley didn't know this captain.

"I've never heard even a rumor—"

"Friends in high places helped her sweep up the pieces of her career and moved her to the fringe," the commander said. "Not many officers are clamoring for an IC route."

"I don't see how that means Gnemo's involved."

"There's rumbles at HQ that she's tired of being banished and was planning something," Gnilsson said. "I was sent to keep an eye on her under the excuse of training for my own command. I could tell she seemed off, but I never thought she'd do something this extreme."

Gnilsson's story was inconceivable. How could the gnome who had made Gnedley learn every page of the procedure manual do something like this? "Why don't we ask her—"

"Would you tell the truth if you were behind this?" Commander Gnilsson pointed at the mushrooms. "I told you. HQ already has their eye on Gnemo. She's got the motive. Plenty of opportunity. You saw how she grabbed first patrol. She must have set this up then. *And* she has the means to move the product. You'd be shocked at the underworld connections our captain has. A payload like this could be her exit strategy."

Gnedley hated how Commander Gnilsson's points were beginning to line up.

"We're walking a dangerous line now. I need your help," Gnilsson said. "This could spell disaster not only for 525-1, but for all other IC planets and the whole of the Alliance."

He leaned forward, staring intently at Gnedley. "Give me some of that faith you put in Gnemo," he said. "If you help me, I can show you the truth about her, the Alliance, and exactly what you've signed up for. Will you do that?"

What Gnedley wanted to do was go back to when his biggest

worry was making sure he labeled his samples correctly. He didn't want to be responsible for this.

But now that he knew, Gnedley had to *know*. If he helped the commander, they would discover who was behind the patch.

If it wasn't Gnemo, they could bring the real culprit to justice and clear her name at HQ.

If it *was* Gnemo—

No one should be able to get away with a crime of this magnitude.

He had his answer. "I'll help you."

"Excellent." Gnilsson stood to pace in front of Gnedley. "Our problem is proof. We'll divide our resources to keep tabs on everything." He tugged at his beard, muttering to himself. "Here's the plan," he said. "I'll watch Gnemo, since I can stick close to her without raising suspicion. Your job is to watch this spot. Keep an eye out for those Humans and report back to me. We need to know what they're up to as well."

He grabbed Gnedley's wrist. "I'm synching your communicator to a private channel connected with mine," Gnilsson said as he pressed a series of buttons on the unit. "If you come across anything, press the call button once, and I'll meet you back at this spot."

Gnedley wondered if he should be writing this down.

That seemed to go against the idea of a secret mission.

Commander Gnilsson sent him a sharp look. "Remember, it's only the two of us stopping this from being an intergalactic disaster."

Gnedley nodded shakily.

No pressure.

CHAPTER 9

"I didn't sign up to be your Trojan horse, Lemon."

"Is it technically a Trojan horse if we're visible?" I pulled Marlo along as she dragged her feet up the sidewalk to Shady Elms. "You're more like our shield. Edie's going to bounce right off you. Metaphorically speaking."

"Why do we need a shield?" Rachel asked.

"Edie is not my biggest fan," I confessed. Marlo snorted. "But she *loves* Marlo." I patted my best friend's shoulder. "Thinks she's a delightful young woman, and we won't ever tell her the truth because it makes for a good distraction. Say hi!"

"Hi, Edie!" she squeaked as I pushed her forward through the doors.

"Hello, Marlo." Nurse Edie came around the desk, headed straight for me. "I see you hiding, Ms. Peabody. What are you up to?"

Well, that plan lasted all of two seconds. "We're here for a quick visit with Grandpa," I said, stepping out from behind Marlo and Rachel. "It's before six p.m.!"

She pursed her lips at our group. "I don't think you need to be trooping in there with a whole gang of friends," she said. "Mr. Peabody needs rest after this morning's outing."

I was getting *real* tired of Nurse Edie putting limitations on my visits with Grandpa. Taking a deep breath, I tamped down most of what I wanted to say. Fighting wouldn't help.

"It'll be quick," I said. "In and out, I promise." I looked to Marlo for some backup.

"Please, Edie?" She smiled sweetly. "I'd really like to say hi to Mr. Peabody."

"Ten minutes," she agreed. "And if I hear any kind of ruckus, I'm coming in there."

"Fine by me." I shot down the hall, Marlo and Rachel following in my wake. Stopping in front of Grandpa's door, I knocked once before going in. "Hey, Grandpa! How's it—"

"*Hhnnnarghhkkk.*"

The man himself snored away in his recliner. Nice to see some things never changed.

"Grandpa," I whispered as I poked at his shoulder. "Wake up."

"Huh, wha—? What?" He startled, grabbing at his glasses and straightening them on his face. Slowly wiping the sleep out of his eyes, he focused on me and smiled. "Hello, dear. Did I know you were coming by today?"

"I wanted to return this and say thanks." I pulled the metal detector out of my bag.

Grandpa Walt frowned slightly. "What did you need the detector for?"

My heart did a funny wobble, but I heard Mom's voice in my head. *"Don't make a big deal when he doesn't remember. Gently give him the information and move on."*

"We borrowed it yesterday for Project Validation." I tucked the detector back into the far corner of his closet and shut the door.

"Of course," he said. "And you brought friends today. Who are these lovely young ladies?" I turned to see him smiling at Marlo and Rachel, who looked over at me hesitantly.

"This is our new friend, Rachel. And you know Marlo." Gentle reminder and move on.

He peered at her. "Marlo?"

"It's me, Mr. Peabody," she said. "I know I look different with the blue hair."

"Oh. I see." He trailed off with a little frown.

Mom was right. Best to keep things going when Grandpa had his little moments. Fluffing things made him frustrated, and I didn't want to dwell on the fact that he was confused by *Marlo*. To be fair, her hair did look bluer now that it was out of yesterday's bun.

Still. She's been coming with me to visit Grandpa since . . . forever.

That's a lot of history to forget.

Marlo coughed and waggled her eyebrows at me. What . . . oh.

"It was a hot summer night," Grandpa was saying to Rachel. "Hotter than it had any right to be, but that's the weather for you—"

"Hey, Grandpa." I jumped in before he got too deep into the retelling. "We've been working on Project Validation and we've hit a wall. I'm hoping you can help."

He perked up, sending a sly smile my way. "Did you find something?"

"We *might* have a lead on the aliens," I said, still reluctant to get his hopes up. "I feel like they're just out of reach, you know? Like I'm always a second behind."

"I didn't find Gnemo," he said. "She found me."

"Right," I said. "In the water."

Grandpa nodded. "Seemed like she appeared out of nowhere. Obviously I was a bit distracted at the time, being on the ground and all."

A kernel of an idea began to form. "Grandpa." I leaned up against his chair. "When Gnemo left," I said, "did you see where she went? Were you able to follow her?"

"No, come to think of it," Grandpa scratched at his chin, mulling that over. "I looked away for a moment, and when I looked back, she was gone. Disappeared into thin air."

Rachel made a small noise. She'd picked up on my brain wave.

Grandpa smiled, glancing over at Marlo and Rachel. "Manners, Lemon," he said. "Are you going to introduce me to your friends?"

Oh. Right. Okay.

I wasn't expecting him to hit the reset button that quickly.

Marlo shot me a concerned look, and Rachel shuffled her feet. I'd prepped Marlo about Grandpa's situation, but I knew experiencing it was a different thing altogether. I wasn't used to it yet myself.

I didn't want to be.

I tried not to let my smile waver. "Of course, Grandpa," I said, patting his shoulder. "These are my friends, Marlo and Rachel. They're helping out with Project Validation."

"Marlo, yes. And welcome, Rachel," Grandpa Walt tapped a finger along the side of his nose. "Come back soon, and we'll break out the good cookies."

I took that as our cue to leave. He wasn't in the right space for any more brainstorming. We could pick it up later. "Thanks for the chat, Grandpa," I said as we moved out the door.

"Anytime, sweetie," He waved us off.

I marched us briskly down the hallway, shooting Marlo a look that said we were *not* talking about this right now. My stomach was twisted in knots, having them see Grandpa's problem laid out so clearly. It felt worse, more real somehow. And if Marlo tried to *talk* to me about it, I was going to lose it.

I needed all of my focus for Project Validation. That was the best thing for everyone.

"Done so soon?" Nurse Edie called as we swept by the desk.

I nodded tightly, not able to bring myself to admit she was right.

Because she wasn't.

She *wasn't*.

"See you, Edie," Marlo said, waving as she followed me and Rachel out onto the sidewalk. "Are you going to tell us the big idea?" she asked as soon as our feet hit pavement. "What part of that story got you two so excited?"

Moving right back to the plan. Marlo was the best.

"Gnemo appeared *out of nowhere*," I said. "And then disappeared. *Without a trace.* What does that make you think of?"

"Oooh, *the shields*!" Marlo said. "You think they've got, like, little portable ones?"

"It makes the most logistical sense," Rachel said. "They need a way to conceal themselves when they leave the ship, and they obviously have the technology."

"Exactly." I powered down the sidewalk, fired up with a new angle for this mission.

"I'm afraid to ask," Marlo said.

"Let them come to us." I grinned. "We stake out spots between the mushrooms and the landing site and set a booby trap. Something to make them *visible* so they can lead us back to the ship."

"You know how to do that?" Rachel cocked her head, squinting at me.

"The internet does."

"Those are the three most terrifying words you've ever said to me," Marlo moaned.

"It'll be fine," I said.

"No, wait." Marlo pointed at me. "*Those* are the worst."

"Just trust me?" I tried.

"You need to stop," she threatened, trying to cover my mouth as I kept laughing.

"The two of you have a strange friendship," Rachel said as she sidestepped our tussle.

We did. Marlo and I smiled at each other. And it was kind of perfect. I bumped shoulders with her as we trailed after Rachel.

"But seriously," I said. "Whose house are we going to? It's research time."

CHAPTER 10

Wednesday morning, we lined up with the rest of the JFR crew, new plan ready to go.

Once Quinn finally *let* us go.

She prowled in front of the group, piercing everyone with their daily dose of ten-seconds-too-long eye contact. A shriek split the air as she blew a sharp note on her whistle.

"It's pervasive," she said. "Insidious. A threat to our entire planet, and it's *your* duty as global citizens to combat it." The pamphlet she thrust into my hands screamed "LITTER KILLS!" across the top and had an illustration of the Earth, with Xs for eyes, lying on top of a trash heap below.

Effective.

"No returning until you've each filled one of these," Quinn

said, handing out large biodegradable garbage bags. "We respect the space nature gives us."

Couldn't have planned a better cover activity myself. Freedom to walk around, setting up our contraptions, and all we had to do was grab garbage along the way. Easy peasy.

Marlo, Rachel, and I hustled into the woods to get to our planned locations. We'd ended up in Marlo's backyard shed last night, away from prying eyes, and hammered out the details.

We were going with the classic trip-wire and bucket setup.

Hang a bucket in the tree. String fishing wire along the ground. Our alien walks into it, snags the wire, and pulls the bucket over. Genius Rachel suggested we fill the buckets with a mixture of watered-down honey and leaves. Her theory was that the honey would mimic sap, so the alien won't question why it dropped from the tree *and* it'll help the leaves stick to the shield.

Ideally, the alien goes back to the ship, and we'll follow to see how they access the wall. And maybe sneak in. *And* hopefully be able to see whether or not Gnemo's with them. Rachel had run us through all the variables of how this might not work, but I had a good feeling.

I dropped my bag at our first spot and started pulling out the buckets and fishing line. The plus side of staying up all night learning how to set trip-wire traps was that I could do this in my sleep. Rachel had the honey mixture, and Marlo was currently gathering up leaves.

After checking sight lines and negotiating the *best* locations, we managed to set up three buckets. One close to the mushrooms, one closer to the clearing, and one smack in the middle. Cover the most ground, divide and conquer, and all that. If anyone's bucket was triggered, they'd use our special signal and the other two would come running. Boom. Success.

Fingers crossed.

Once Marlo and Rachel were set, I hunkered down in my own spot—the middle ground. Fluffing up some ferns around me, I crouched behind a tree. And sat.

And waited.

I slapped at a bug eyeing up my skin.

My legs were falling asleep, but I didn't want to stretch and give away my location. I jiggled one knee. Then the other. No signal from Marlo or Rachel yet. How long had we been here? I pulled out my phone to check the time.

Five. Minutes.

Wow, stakeouts were boring. No wonder the aliens never showed up to Grandpa's. I wonder if he—

What was that?

I kept perfectly still and heard the rustling noise again. Looking around, I scanned through the trees and saw a cluster of tall grass swaying even though there was no wind. Bobbing like something had brushed past it. Or someone.

A few more feet to the left, and it would hit my trip wire.

Come ooooooooooon.

The wire pushed forward, pulling on the line running up the tree, tipping over the bucket. *Splash.*

The honey-and-leaf mixture rained down, streaming around the sides of *something* about three feet tall.

"There you are," I whispered.

There was a flurry of leaf movement as the invisible figure tried to wipe off the mess, but it was a losing battle. A quiet huff of breath, then the leaf pile started to move away from me. Quickly.

Too quickly.

I had to move fast if I was going to see where they went and if they revealed themselves. My fingers felt numb as I fumbled to grab my bag, stand up, and sling it over my shoulder at the same time.

I tried to keep to the trees without losing sight of the pile of leaves zipping through the air, but one by one the leaves started falling to the ground. This was no time for stealth. My body kicked into gear before my brain and sped up to give chase.

"What are you doing?" Marlo whispered as I ran past.

Oh, yeah. The signal.

"Caw!" I yelled over my shoulder. "Caw! *Caw!*"

My legs burned as I willed them to go faster. Whoever this was, they were quick.

But the distance between us was closing.

Marlo and Rachel crashed along behind me. The patch of leaves took a sharp turn, but I was catching up—until my foot hit a root and I fell forward, arms out, accidentally taking the mystery figure down to the ground with me. We grunted. There was a sudden flicker, and I caught sight of a bit of green and red before it disappeared again.

Was it really—

"Gnemo?" I whispered.

The invisible figure jerked in my arms, pushing me away. Hard.

The world went off-kilter as I fell back to the ground, and I groaned at the sound of footsteps running away as fast as they could.

Marlo and Rachel burst out from behind a tree at high speed, unable to hit the brakes. I urged my tired jelly legs to move, but they wouldn't budge even as my friends hurtled into me. The three of us lay on the ground in a tangle.

"That failed miserably," Rachel moaned, pulling herself out of the pile.

"No, I caught a glimpse," I said, panting for breath. "I think they might've been Gnemo."

"But we don't know for sure," Marlo said. "Because you abandoned the plan and freaking chased an alien through the woods. What? Was that?"

"I couldn't stop myself." I scrubbed a hand over my face, wiping away the sweat. "The leaves were falling off and the idea of losing track of them was too much. It just happened."

"What do we do now?" Rachel asked, plucking a sticky leaf off her arm.

"Well, we lost the element of surprise, thanks to me." I tried to fight down worries that I'd destroyed our progress with one impulsive chase. "I guess we come up with a new plan?"

A flash on the ground hit my eyes as sunlight streamed through the trees.

Taking a closer look, I smiled. Not exactly what I'd hoped for, but still a win. "Look." I held out my find for Rachel and Marlo to examine.

It was a small black rectangle, similar to a tablet, covered with symbols I didn't recognize. Except for one. On the back was a very familiar leaf.

"The same symbol." Rachel bent over to take a closer look. "Maybe it represents their culture, or an organization?"

Marlo's mouth dropped open. "What do you think it is?"

"No idea." I grinned. "Want to try to find out?"

Gnedley

The Human had called him *Gnemo*!

Commander Gnilsson was right. The captain *had* met with these IC inhabitants.

Did that mean he was right about everything else?

Gnedley didn't want to think about that. Or his other problem.

The Human had seen his *face*.

Curse that sticky substance from the tree. It had covered his shield when it rained down, making him visible to the very Humans he'd been looking for.

Who then *chased* him!

Their tumble had jostled his shield badge and the faulty thing shorted out, only for a second, but that was enough.

Gnedley had seen the look on the Human's face. He knew the Human had seen his.

What a mess.

He should return to the ship and hand in his uniform. He was a disgrace to the Alliance. Gnedley patted his pockets for his logbook so he could draft his resignation. Where—

His logbook was gone. Dropped during the chase.

Great Gnominium, this was a full-fledged disaster.

He fumbled for his wrist, pressing the call button on his communicator. Hopefully Commander Gnilsson would be able to head back to the patch quickly. Gnedley broke into a run and made sure to give the trees a wide berth. If he was going to keep making mistakes, he could at least not make the same one twice.

He skidded to a stop near one of the stumps.

"Commander?" he whispered. *"Commander?"*

"What's happened, Ensign?" Gnilsson popped into sight after three more panic-inducing seconds. "Has someone else accessed the mushrooms? Did you locate the Humans?"

"It's an emergency," Gnedley said as he turned off his shield. The whole story came tumbling out in a flood—the Humans, the chase, and his lost logbook.

"They knew the captain's name," he said, loath to accept the implications of that.

"She must have made contact," Gnilsson concluded. "I believe they're working together."

"Can we really be certain—"

"For now," Gnilsson said, "we have to proceed as though the captain is compromised. She can't be trusted."

Gnedley couldn't even begin to think of what to do next. This was extraordinarily overwhelming.

Commander Gnilsson clapped a firm hand on his shoulder. "I'll guard the patch for now . . . if you can manage one very important task."

"Yes," Gnedley said. Anything to clean up his part in this mess and make things right.

"Find those Humans," Gnilsson said. "Recover your logbook and investigate whether they have any mushrooms in their possession."

"H-How?" Gnedley stammered. "I wouldn't even know where to begin."

"Our logs are trackable," the commander reminded him, pointing at a small scanner on Gnedley's belt. "Keying in your passcode will provide you with coordinates."

"You won't come too?" Gnedley unclipped the scanner with a shaking hand.

"Gnemo's expecting me later," he said. "She'll ask questions if we're both late. You're new. We can say you got lost."

Gnedley's stomach turned at the thought of exploiting the captain's trust. But this was the only way to get his logbook back . . . and get some answers.

He desperately needed answers.

Gnedley nodded, squaring his shoulders. He was a member of the *Alliance*. He could outwit these Humans and put their mission back on track.

"That's the attitude, sprout," Gnilsson said. "Stay calm and be smart out there." He paused. "Well, *smarter*."

Not the vote of confidence Gnedley had hoped for.

"Keep your shield up at all times," Gnilsson said. "And take this." He held out his laser pruner. They had a few onboard for tough-to-get samples, but Gnedley had no use for it now.

"For protection," the commander said, pressing it into Gnedley's hand.

"A weapon?" Gnedley shook his head, giving it back. These weren't hardened pirates he was dealing with. They were Humans. Young ones.

"You'll truly be on your own out there, Ensign. You don't know—"

"No, thank you, sir," Gnedley said firmly.

"Suit yourself." The commander shook his head, disappearing as he activated his own shield.

And as he had said, Gnedley was on his own.

"You wanted to see more of the planet," Gnedley reminded himself. He typed his passcode into the scanner, prompting coordinates and a map to pop up on the screen.

"Easy enough."

He started forward, watching the map carefully as he went. With a sudden gasp, he stopped when a small, fluffy gray creature approached. The . . . what was the Human classification? . . . *squirrel* stopped to stare at him with curious eyes. Gnedley peered back, seeing his own reflection—

His *reflection*. He hadn't activated his shield badge.

Gnedley slapped at the button, willing his shield to turn on, and braced a hand against his hearts when the safeguard sprang into place.

"Yeah." He sighed. "Easy."

CHAPTER 11

As I turned the tablet in my hands, a shiver ran down my spine. I was holding an actual piece of alien technology.

"Wild idea here." Marlo pointed at the tablet. "This is solid proof," she said. "Won't your dad believe you now?"

Could it be that easy? I tried viewing the tablet through a more suspicious gaze.

"Aside from the weird buttons, it looks like a regular tablet. He'll think it's fake," I said. "And getting Dad to believe is only part of it. I want to reunite Grandpa and Gnemo if we can."

I held up the tablet. "If we can figure out how this works, maybe it'll get us past the shield and into the ship?" Thank goodness we had a scientist onboard now. I grinned at Rachel. "How do we science this thing? Poke all the buttons?"

"First we take it to a secure location," she said, all business. "For examination."

That ruled out my house. Marlo rolled her eyes at my look. "We can go to my place."

"Excellent." I stuffed the tablet into my bag, eager to get going. "Then what?"

Rachel tilted her head, considering the options. "Then we poke all the buttons and see what happens."

I loved science.

Rachel headed home to ask if she could sleep over, Marlo went to make sure we *could* sleep over, and me—I had an important stop on the way to my own house.

Jogging up to the retirement home, I noticed a familiar figure lurking by the shrubbery.

"Sully," I called, and he shushed me frantically, shoving something crinkly into his pocket while casting a quick look at the front door.

Ooh. Shenanigans. "Whatcha got there?"

"A person's entitled to their secrets, young lady," he said sternly.

I stared him down until he pulled the corner of a chip bag out of his pocket. "Staff's been harping about my cholesterol, so I'm hiding in the bushes to eat my snack in peace."

"Sorry to interrupt."

"Eh, I'm done." He offered his arm. "Milady?"

I swung mine to link up as we walked in and blinked at the empty desk.

"Edie's off sick," Sully explained. "Her fill-in's doing rounds."

"Lucky for me." My grin faded as we walked down the hallway and the low hum of background noise gave way to the sound of agitated voices in Grandpa's room. I shot a look at Sully, confused.

"Sounds like Walt's having an off day," he said with a wince. "New staff throws him. It's better when things are familiar."

An *off day*? Dad talked about Grandpa having those, but I figured that was because putting the two of them together wasn't going to end well *any* day. A shout had me pushing into the room.

"Mr. Peabody, please." A tall nurse in blue scrubs stood beside Grandpa Walt's chair, hands on her hips. "You have to take your medication before dinner."

"I said no." Grandpa Walt sat rigidly in his seat. "Who are you? Where's Edie?"

The nurse took a breath. "I'm Carolyn," she said in an even tone. "I was here this morning and at lunch. I'm covering for Edie today."

"I don't like strangers in my room," he said, volume rising again. "Get out—"

"Grandpa!" I'd never heard him speak to anyone that way. They both jumped at the sound of my voice, and I hurried over. "Are you okay?"

"Lemon," he said, patting my arm with a shaky hand. "Did I know you were coming by?"

"Surprise visit," I said. "Sounds like you're getting a lot of those today."

The new nurse gave me a tight smile. "As I said, Edie's out sick, so I'm covering her rounds and I have a number of patients to get to before the end of my shift."

Never let it be said that Lemon Peabody couldn't take a hint. "Who knew Nurse Edie could get sick? I thought she was a cyborg for sure, eh, Grandpa?"

Carolyn snorted the snort of someone well acquainted with Edie. "I need to take your blood pressure, then I can give you your pills and get out of your hair," she said to Grandpa.

He wrenched his arm away, scowling at her.

"Hey!" I poked at him. "Why are you being so grumpy?"

"She's the one who came in here uninvited," Grandpa Walt muttered.

This from the guy who loved visitors. Grandpa Walt would

chat with anybody about anything. Or he used to. I was losing track of what was usual.

"She's here to help," I said, patting his shoulder. "Like Edie." Even though it pained me to say it.

Grandpa grumbled but let Carolyn finish up her visit. Sully, who'd been lingering in the doorway, slipped out as well.

I settled on the footstool beside Grandpa's chair. "That wasn't so bad, right?"

He leaned back, still looking a little bothered, and to be honest, I felt rattled too. I'd *never* seen him behave like that. Grandpa Walt usually had a smile for everyone.

"Do you really not remember her stopping by before?" I blurted out. It sounded like she'd been in a few times.

Grandpa waved off my concern. "Must not have had my glasses on," he said. "People's faces blend together." He shrugged. "Heck of a thing, getting old."

"You were pretty cranky," I said. "She might tattle on you to Edie."

"I'll apologize," he promised, shrinking down into his seat. He looked sad and dulled in a way that made my stomach clench. Grandpa had always had a sparkle in his eye, but lately it seemed like the spark kept on wavering.

Luckily, I had the perfect thing to cheer him up. "Guess what?" I drummed my hands against my legs.

His lips twitched. "Chicken butt?"

There. He was perking up, and I hadn't even opened my bag yet. I reached inside to pull out the tablet. "We think we spotted an alien in the woods today,"

Grandpa sat at full attention. "Was it Gnemo? Did you talk to her?"

"I'm not sure *who* it was," I said, setting the tablet in his lap. "We lost them, but they dropped this." Cupping my chin in my hands, I grinned.

"Amazing." Grandpa Walt turned the tablet over, inspecting every inch. "What is it?"

"I have no idea!" I beamed at him. "Isn't it cool?"

"Remarkable," he said, running a finger over the back of the tablet. "This symbol . . ."

"Do you recognize it?"

"Would you grab the gnome from beside my bed, please?" Grandpa Walt looked lost in thought. "I want to check something," he said softly.

I ran to the bedroom, grabbed the gnome, and was back at his chair in two seconds flat.

He took the figurine out of my hands, turning it over slowly. "Your grandmother was always working on one art project or another," he said. "She made me this after I met Gnemo."

"Really?" I had no idea. I wondered if Dad knew.

"Said I needed a place to keep my memories and . . ." Grandpa Walt grabbed the gnome's cap, twisting until it popped off to reveal a hidden compartment. "This." He gently reached in to show me what was inside.

"Wow," I whispered.

It was a small green leaf, no longer than my pinkie finger. The green was so bright, it looked like it was glowing in his hand.

"May I?"

Grandpa nodded, holding it out.

I picked it up, laying a careful stroke along the top. It was velvety soft. The scent was like the best day in spring, when everything's fresh and starting to grow.

And it was shaped exactly like the symbol on the tablet. And the metal plates.

"Is this from Gnemo?"

"Gave it to me before she left," Grandpa said. "I think she wanted me to have something to remember her by, but she also said it would help keep me safe if I ever ran into another alien."

All these years. It should be a dried-up pile of leaf dust by now, but it looked freshly plucked from a tree.

"I was never sure if I believed in aliens," he said. "Never gave it any thought, but since that night, I've known there's more out there than I'll ever get to see."

"You got a pretty amazing souvenir out of it."

Grandpa stopped me when I tried to place the leaf back in its hiding spot. "Keep it."

"Oh, Grandpa, I couldn't—"

"We both know I can't go running around in the woods anymore, Lemon," he said. "I know you won't stop until you find them, so if they're really back, with or without Gnemo, I want you to be protected."

"I'll keep it safe," I promised, tucking the leaf into my pocket.

"Keep yourself safer." He gave me a solemn look as he put the cap back in place and set the gnome on his side table.

"I'm going to find Gnemo." I believed it now more than ever.

"It'd be nice to have one last chat," he said wistfully.

"Talk about the secrets of the universe again?"

"Yeah." Grandpa Walt smiled, but his eyes were far away, looking into the past. Edie might have a point about keeping visits short and sweet.

I grabbed the tablet and stuffed it back in my bag before giving him a squeeze. "Love you to the moon and more, Grandpa." I kissed his cheek and headed for the door.

Time to science.

CHAPTER 12

I burst through our front door, kicked off my shoes, and ran up the stairs. "Going to a sleepover at Marlo's!"

Mom emerged from the bathroom, jolting as I whizzed past her on the landing. "How about 'May I go to a sleepover at Marlo's?'"

I paused in my doorway. "May I sleep over at Marlo's? Pleeeeeeeeease?" Zooming over to the dresser, I started shoving clothes into a bag.

"Yes, as long as Sofía and Allison have agreed." Mom came in to perch on the end of my bed. "You seem awfully excited for something you do on a regular basis."

Uh-oh. That was her "What's Lemon up to?" voice. I sneaked a peek over my shoulder. "Our new friend from

Junior Forest Rangers is coming too."

"Oh?"

Aha. Now I had her.

"Rachel, the girl I told you about yesterday," I said. "We thought it'd be fun to immerse her in the full Lemon-and-Marlo-friendship experience."

Mom hummed softly. "That's great, sweetie. I'm glad you and Marlo are expanding your circle a little."

Expanding our . . . "What's *that* mean?" I muttered as I attempted to stuff my pillow into the bag.

"You and Marlo are very good friends." Mom helpfully held the sides open so I could cram in the last corner. "But you don't have to be each other's *only* friends."

I was tempted to pull out the chart Marlo and I had made in third grade, outlining exactly why we're the perfect pair of friends, but that seemed counterproductive when her concern for my social skills was netting me a sleepover pass.

"You're right," I said. "Rachel's cool. She's already taught me a ton about science and nature." I zipped the bag shut, slinging it over my shoulder. "Can't wait to return the favor and teach her everything *I* know."

A faint frown line creased her forehead. "What's Rachel's last name again?"

"Morris. Why?"

Mom headed out the door. "I should contact her parents and give them a heads-up."

"Hah," I called after her. Rachel would *be* so lucky to learn the ins and outs of my skill sets. I shoved a few more supplies into my bag and headed downstairs.

"See you tomorrow!" I hollered before dashing over to Marlo's house.

Rachel was waiting on the front porch, a bag on her back and a tote box hugged to her chest. A tall man with deep brown skin and a shy smile mirroring Rachel's stood beside her as he chatted with Sofía.

"Here she is," Sofía said. "Lemon, this is Mr. Morris, Rachel's dad."

"The famous Lemon." Rachel's dad nodded. "Please call me Luke. I've heard so much about you and Marlo."

"Daaaaaaad," Rachel groaned under her breath.

"It's nice to meet you," he said, ignoring Rachel, brown eyes crinkling up behind wire-rimmed glasses. He reached out to shake my hand, and I returned it with three enthusiastic pumps. No more. No less. Learned that from Sully.

Mr. Morris—Luke's lips quirked as he released my hand. "How are you enjoying Junior Forest Rangers?"

"It's great," I replied. "Feels like I'm really getting to experience nature. It's good stuff."

"Glad to hear it." He laughed and swept an arm around Rachel for a hug. "Have fun, baby. Love you."

"Bye, dad! Love you too." She followed me down the steps as I waved my goodbyes, and we headed through the gate to the backyard.

"Your folks give you any trouble over the sleepover?" I asked Rachel.

"No," she said with a surprised shrug. "Turns out my mom works with Sofía at the university, and they've talked about a get-together for a while. They did wonder why I was bringing this." She raised the tote in her hands. "But I told them it was part of a JFR project."

"Mushrooms?" I whispered with a nod at the tote.

"I thought we could add them to tonight's study?"

"What else are science sleepovers for?" I grinned.

Allison and Marlo were in the backyard setting up the tent. Or to be specific, Allison was setting up the tent while Marlo battled to stick one of the poles in the ground.

"Are you sure you didn't lose pieces during your last trip? This one isn't right," Marlo complained. "It won't fit."

"Not sure the piece is the problem," Allison said, keeping her distance as Marlo stabbed at the grass.

"Don't see why we need a tent when we could sleep in my room," Marlo grumbled after spotting us. "You know, *inside*."

"Because *adventure*!" I tried to silently remind her we needed to be outside with extra privacy so no one walked in on us attempting to science the tablet. And now the mushrooms too.

"Why are you looking at me like that?" Marlo straightened up, clenching her hands on her hips. Oh, for Pete's sake. Whatever happened to the best friend psychic connection?

"Staying inside might be better," Allison said, dubiously eyeing Marlo's side of the tent.

"We *have* to sleep outside because—" Think, Lemon, think.

"We need to finish our constellation worksheet for Junior Forest Rangers," Rachel said.

Welcome to the team, Rachel! I pointed a triumphant finger at her. "Yes, we have important *star* work to do. Right, Marlo?"

"Right." Understanding flooded her face. "I forgot about the important star work."

"If you're sure." Allison laughed. "Let's finish setting this up. Grab that side, Lemon."

Between the four of us, we got the tent up, and Allison headed back into the house. I turned to Rachel. "High fives on the assignment thing! That was great."

She tapped my hand, grinning. "You know, we *could* do some constellation work. It's supposed to be clear tonight, and I've always wanted to map the path of—"

"Star mapping sounds great, and we will absolutely do that," I said, unzipping my bag and pulling out the tablet. "But first we have to tackle *this*."

"Inside." Marlo held the tent flap open for us to file through.

Once we were seated cross-legged in the tent, I set the tablet down in the middle of our circle. "What should we press first?"

"The power button?" Marlo suggested. "Or something that looks like a home button?"

"If I was an alien power button, where would I be?" I peered at the tablet.

"I'm just going to try one." Rachel reached out a tentative finger.

"Yeah, okay," I said, pushing it toward her. "Get in there."

Her hand hovered over the tablet for a moment before she struck, lightning quick, and jabbed at the largest button.

We bent our heads together and stared, waiting for something to happen.

Nothing.

"Hmm." I pressed *all* the buttons, one after another, for good measure.

Still nothing.

"Think the battery died?" I gave it a little wiggle.

Rachel rested her chin in her hand. "Maybe it's fingerprint activated?"

"That would be . . . extremely inconvenient," I said.

"Did you try asking for advice in any of your alien hunter forums?" Marlo asked.

"Alien *tracker* forums, and no," I said. "I didn't want to risk a frenzy and have people trying to pin us down to see the tech."

"Good call," Marlo said. "But now what?"

I turned to our resident scientist. "Keep poking?"

Rachel nodded. "Keep poking."

After supper and many hours of poking the tablet later, everyone lay half asleep in the tent. Once we'd tried every possible point of access—short of cracking it open like Rachel suggested—we decided to give our brains a break.

The rest of the night was spent helping Rachel process mushroom samples and learning about the ways she would try to cultivate them. The many disgusting-sounding but interesting ways.

Marlo read us the beginning of her goose murder mystery, which was amazing, of course, but also chockful of nightmare material. I still couldn't believe how freaky geese are.

Then, to Rachel's delight, we did a bit of star mapping.

Our delight too. Constellations are cool.

"This was fun," Rachel said as we got ready for bed. She

wrapped her hair in a silky light blue scarf and climbed into her sleeping bag.

"You sound surprised," Marlo said, pulling a chunky sweatshirt over her head. She had a thing about always being cold at night outside, even in the summer.

"I wasn't sure what to expect," Rachel explained. "We've never hung out before."

"In the morning, there'll be pancakes," I said, fluffing up my special pillow. "I wrangled a promise out of Allison."

"Pancakes are good," Rachel confirmed solemnly. You had to appreciate someone who took a quality breakfast seriously.

"Good night, friends," Marlo said, clicking off the flashlight, and I caught the little smile on Rachel's face before we plunged into darkness.

It *was* a good night. Rachel fit right in with our long-standing team of two.

Mom might be on to something with this whole widening-the-circle thing.

I went to bed satisfied with our efforts. Tomorrow was a new day, and we'd figure it out eventually. My only worry was how long eventually might actually be.

I rolled over in my sleeping bag and stared at the tablet, barely visible in the dark. How many secrets did it hold? What wonders were we about to unlock?

A rustle outside the tent caught my attention. I held still, trying to make sense of the shadows splashed across the walls. Was that a little triangle bobbing along? Maybe . . . a cat's ear?

Ooh! Wade!

Allison always let him into the yard to get his ya-yas out before bedtime. She said it was better for him to run off his energy outside than up and down the hallway. I chuckled to myself.

This was my moment. Get ready for some serious cuddles, Wade.

Slithering out of my sleeping bag, I gathered it up and crept over to the tent flap. I held my breath and willed the zipper to be silent as I brought it down as slowly as humanly possible. The rustling grew louder and the shadow crept closer.

When it rounded the corner, I leaped out of the tent, sleeping bag in hand.

"Ahahahahah!" I cried victoriously. "Snuggle up, Wade!"

The trapped beast began to struggle. Really struggle. "This is the opposite of snuggling." I tightened my grasp and felt something a lot bigger than a cat.

Pressing down on the thrashing bundle, I peeled back the top of the sleeping bag.

And gasped.

"You're not Wade," I said to the shocked green face staring back at me.

Gnedley

What the—

CHAPTER 13

"Oh my gosh. Oh my gosh. Oh my gooooooosh."

Marlo maintained a constant stream of panic as she flung open the door of the shed while Rachel and I hauled the wriggling sleeping bag inside. I wasn't feeling exactly calm myself.

"This is unreal," she gasped. "Oh my gosh."

I pushed garden tools out of the way with my foot, punctuating Marlo's hyperventilating with clangs and grunts. It was dark and musty inside, but farther away from the house than our tent. And it had a proper door. All the better to hide our current *situation*.

I crashed against a wall as the being in my arms flexed and flailed.

"We seriously have to keep it down," Marlo hissed, closing the door behind us. She flicked on the hanging lamp with a soft click, and a murky light filled the room. Aside from the tools, there was a workbench and a lawn mower. "We can't wake up my parents."

"You're the one who's going to wake them," I whispered.

Mumbled outrage came from Rachel's end. "Not to interrupt, but . . ." she said, sending a significant glance down at our squirming bundle.

"Over there," I said, directing my head at the workbench along the back wall. We shuffled over and set the sleeping bag down, leaning the top end against the bench.

The three of us leaped back as whoever was inside flailed their way out. A crumpled red hat emerged, followed by a very disgruntled green face. Silence filled the shed as the three of us stared in shock.

"That's an alien," Marlo said.

My cheeks ached at the grin cracking my face. "I know."

"No," Marlo said. "That. Is. An. *Alien*." She took a shaky step back, eyes wide, and I didn't get it. This was the plan. The whole deal. Why was she freaking out? Did she—

"Did you not *believe* me?" My own best friend.

"I . . . I did?" She shook her head. "I totally did, but . . ." Marlo blew out a breath. "I need a minute to process. Talk amongst yourselves."

I turned to Rachel. "You need to process?"

"All good," she said, staring in fascination.

"I'm gonna dive in." I sat down in front of our guest. "We mean you no harm," I said slowly, showing my hands.

Marlo snorted and I shot her a look. "Is that the sound of you being done processing?"

"No, but I think you need the help," she said, sitting beside me and turning to the alien. "Do you speak English?"

That was an idea. "Parlez-vous français?"

The alien looked down, pressing their lips together in a firm line.

"¿Hablas español?" Marlo tried.

Still nothing.

"Do you know any other languages?" I asked Rachel.

"I'm only fluent in science," she said with a shrug. "Do you want to talk spore-bearing fruit bodies?"

The alien's eyes skated over to Rachel.

"Is that why you're here?" Excitement crept into her voice as she sat by my other side. "For science?"

They stared at their lap in stony silence.

Time for a new tactic. "Where are our manners? We should introduce ourselves," I said. "I'm Lemon Peabody. This gal is my best friend of eight hundred years—"

"She means eight."

"Marlo García-Reynolds. And this is our new friend,

Rachel Morris. She's also our resident scientist, so I think you could be friends too." I put on my most winning smile, and the alien shot me a wary glance. Progress?

"Are you Gnemo? Do you know Gnemo?"

The alien's head shot up as they sucked in a panicked breath.

"Whoa," Marlo said. "It's okay." She leaned in to whisper at me. "I think we're scaring them."

The solution hit like a lightning bolt. "I know what we need," I said, clambering up to my feet. "Please stay," I begged the alien. "I'll be right back."

I zipped to the tent in record time. Rifling through my bag's inner pocket, I gently pulled out Grandpa Walt's leaf from where I'd tucked it for safekeeping.

Perfect.

I grabbed the tablet too, in case it had some kind of translation capability, and ran back to the shed. Sitting down beside the alien, I offered both items with shaking hands.

"You're safe here," I said. "We only want to talk."

The alien snatched the tablet out of my hand before they gaped at the leaf. They spoke rapidly in a language I didn't recognize. Before I could even begin to worry about translating, a slightly tinny voice echoed throughout the shed, like music to my ears.

"Where did you get that?"

Gnedley

Gnedley's world was turning upside down.

With a single gesture, this Human—Lemon Peabody—made him question everything he'd ever been told. Gnedley stared at the luminous green leaf in her hands.

"Where did you get that?"

She narrowed her eyes at him. "You recognize it?"

Gnedley was leery of giving away too much information, but if he wanted answers, he didn't have much choice. A *little* information couldn't hurt.

"Yes," he said.

"Care to elaborate?" Lemon Peabody sighed at his silence, picking up the leaf and twirling it by the stem. "If you tell us where it's from, I'll tell you how I got it."

A trade then. And considering how urgently he wished to know how she'd acquired that leaf, this was a trade he could live with.

"It's from a tree on my planet called the gnomad," he said. "If you detach a leaf during the apex of its life cycle, it stays green forever. We give them to other planets when treaties are ratified. The tree is known as a symbol of peace."

Gnedley nodded toward the leaf. "It's tradition on my planet to give one to a family member before their first mission. For safe travels."

"That's what I was told it's for," Lemon Peabody said with a small smile.

"The tradition spread," Gnedley agreed. "Many other planets in . . . our organization took up the custom, making it an intergalactic symbol of goodwill. How did it come into *your* possession, Lemon Peabody?"

"Call me Lemon." She carefully tucked the leaf away in her pocket. "As for how I got it—whew, I guess I should start at the beginning? Okay, so, it was a hot summer night. Hotter than it had any right to be, but that's the weather for you. . . ."

"Then Grandpa Walt gave *me* the leaf, and here we are."

Gnedley slumped against the table, mind whirling. Lemon's story was *nothing* like what Commander Gnilsson had said. She talked about the Gnemo that Gnedley knew. The one who would never put an Isolated Community in danger for her own gain.

"I'm guessing you're not Gnemo." Lemon regarded him closely. "What *is* your name?"

"Gnedley," he said. "I'm an ensign on Captain Gnemo's ship—"

"Gnemo's a captain now?" she squealed. "Wow. Wait until Grandpa Walt hears."

"That's a great name," Marlo said. "Hey, Gnedley, we also use something called pronouns on our planet. Do you know what those are? Do you use anything like them?"

He flipped through his mental files for the terms Humans used on 525-1, pleased to have brushed up before their crash landing. "You may use 'he.'"

The one called Rachel Morris was practically vibrating as she watched everything unfold. Gnedley looked over at her. "Did you also have a question?"

"What's translating your language into English as you speak?" The words burst out of her as she scooched forward.

"An implant, here," Gnedley said, pointing behind his right ear. "Translates anything spoken to me. And this"—he patted a black circle near his faulty shield badge—"translates my replies into the speaker's language. It has all of the known dialects we've cataloged from the universe, but more are added all the time. We also have a scanner and projector for translating visual communication."

"You could speak to anyone, anywhere on our planet?" Rachel asked.

Gnedley nodded. "On this planet and beyond."

"That's so cool," Lemon said. "What about you? Any questions for us?"

Any questions? Try hundreds. Rachel Morris was not the only individual trembling with excitement. A chance to speak with residents of an IC planet? A once-in-a-lifetime opportunity.

The need to follow protocol battled with his curiosity.

Captain Gnemo did it, a small voice in the back of his mind said. Why couldn't Gnedley?

"I have *so many questions*," he gasped, and Lemon laughed in delight.

"Here's a mutually beneficial idea," she said, tapping her chin and glancing at the other two Humans. "Would you like to join our science sleepover?"

"Yes, gladly," Gnedley said. "What's that?"

CHAPTER 14

"You're gonna love it," I said to Gnedley. "But we need more supplies. Can you stay here for a minute? We'll be right back."

Gnedley nodded, cozying into the sleeping bag, and I ushered Marlo and Rachel out to the tent. We needed to grab our stuff so *we* could get comfortable—but first a private discussion.

We huddled up inside the tent. "Okay," I said. "Alien in the shed. Willing to share information. How much are we sharing? The Grandpa-Gnemo-leaf story was one thing, but—"

"Not the mushrooms," Rachel said immediately. "He might take them away, and I'm not done studying them."

"We probably shouldn't completely trust him yet," Marlo agreed.

"What about stealth questions, to see if he knows about them?" I suggested.

"Let Rachel ask," Marlo said. She held up a hand, cutting off my protests. "Lemon, of the three of us, you are the least stealthy. Like level one stealth skills."

"I can be stealthy when it counts," I muttered.

"Moving on," Marlo said. "Does that plan work for you, Rachel?"

She nodded. Plan settled, we gathered the rest of our sleeping bags and a few more snacks before returning to the shed. A small furry shape slipped through the door as it opened, making a beeline for Gnedley.

He looked up in surprise. "A feline!"

"That's Wade." Marlo laughed. "I think he likes you."

"Hello, Feline Wade." Gnedley smiled at his lapful of cat and scritched Wade behind the ears. Then Wade—the betrayer—*purred*.

"What happened to stranger danger, Wade?" I hissed.

"They have a history," Marlo explained to a very confused Gnedley. "Don't worry about it, you're fine."

Apparently finer than me in the eyes of Wade.

The three of us settled on the floor around Gnedley, and I tossed the last of the snacks into the middle of our circle. I grinned at his discreet sniffing of the open bag of marshmallows. "Want to try one? Help yourself."

"Captain Gnemo says we shouldn't eat anything that hasn't been scanned and tested."

"Yeah, I guess that makes sense—"

Gnedley snatched a marshmallow and it disappeared into his mouth.

I couldn't help the giggle when his eyes went wide. "Good?"

He nodded profusely.

"Have as many as you want," I said, nudging the bag in his direction.

Gnedley swallowed and dug around in a pouch connected to his belt. He pulled out a fuzzy green clump. "One of our snacks." He offered it with a small smile. "Moss from home. It travels well and is very nutritious."

Adventure, right? We each grabbed a little chunk and I popped mine into my mouth, chewing thoughtfully. "This tastes familiar," I said to Marlo.

"Mmm-mm-mmmm." She waved a hand at me as she swallowed. "Like the cucumber-mint water when my moms do spa day, but chewy!"

"Yes!" I turned to Gnedley. "It's delicious. Thank you."

Rachel hummed her agreement, and his small smile spread into a full grin.

I gasped. "That was our first cultural exchange!"

"I should make note of this." Gnedley picked up the tablet, and that reminded me.

"Sorry, by the way, for swiping your, uh . . ."

"Logbook," he supplied as he pressed a thumb to one of the buttons. Rachel stilled, and he noticed her watchful eye. "It has a biometric lock."

"I knew it," she whispered. Shaking her arm with a wince, Rachel turned it to display a nasty scrape across her elbow.

"You're injured," Gnedley said.

"I think it happened when . . ."

When we were lugging him into the shed. Oops.

"This will help." Gnedley reached into another pocket, retrieving what looked like a small light green bandage. "If I may?"

Rachel gave her permission, and he carefully pressed it against her scratch.

"It's warming up." She made a surprised noise as the bandage morphed from green to brown, seamlessly matching Rachel's skin and smoothing out until it disappeared.

"What? Why . . . how is it healed?" Rachel couldn't ask her questions fast enough.

"It's a synthesized replica of the skin of a shape-shifting worm from my planet," Gnedley said. "We discovered the healing properties of the worm could be grafted onto other creatures with no ill effects. One bandage goes a long way, and on a space voyage, fast-acting treatments requiring minimal storage space are highly prized."

Rachel continued grilling him, and my thoughts wandered while Gnedley answered patiently. There was more to the aliens than I'd ever dreamed possible. The shields were impressive, but their medicine was off the charts. If they had access to that kind of knowledge—

My heart thudded in my chest.

Maybe . . .

Maybe they could help Grandpa.

I doubted sticking one of those bandages on his head would do the trick, but if their technology could instantly heal a cut . . . there *had* to be so much more they could do.

"Of course the information shared within the Alliance greatly increases our database," Gnedley was saying.

"What's the Alliance?" Rachel asked, and I tuned back in. I needed all of the details to figure out what possibilities might now be open to us.

"Where to start?" He grabbed another marshmallow and chewed, contemplating his answer. "I'm from a planet called Gnome," he said. "It's many, *many* light years from here and has the greenest hills, the tallest woods, and the pinkest oceans. I've seen countless amazing planets on this journey, but Gnome will always be the most beautiful."

"Pinkest oceans," Rachel mouthed.

"Gnome is a founding member of the Interplanetary Natural Archives Alliance. The Alliance, for short," Gnedley continued, tucking his logbook into his lap. "Our mission is to catalog all life in the universe. We take samples and make records for every single species and habitat. If you think your planet is vast, imagine that multiplied across galaxies."

"Whew." I blew out a breath. "That's a big job."

Gnedley nodded earnestly. "Each piece of data gathered is logged into the central archive on our planet—the Gnomenclature. It will never be complete as long as there's life to be studied."

"Why?" Marlo asked. "Why do all of that work?"

"For science," Gnedley and Rachel replied in unison. She smiled as Gnedley chuckled.

"Because every planet teaches us new skills and perspectives," he said. "The more we learn, the more we all grow."

"It sounds like an honorable mission," Rachel said, pausing to consider her next words. "So why keep hidden? Why not introduce yourselves to Earth? People would love to learn and have access to all of that information."

"Would they, though?" Gnedley shook his head as she

started to argue. "I'm sure there are some, but can you honestly say *all* would welcome a visit from beings from another planet?"

We definitely could not say that.

"Every planet in the Alliance is capable of universal exploration themselves. They were aware of life outside of their own world before joining. The desire to know more drove their technological advances," Gnedley said. "But not every planet progresses at the same rate. There are others, such as your planet, that are what we call IC planets, or Isolated Communities."

Marlo wrinkled her nose. "That sounds a bit culty."

"'Sheltered' would be a better term," Gnedley said. "And not a negative one. It simply means your planet doesn't yet have contact with communities outside its own and the Alliance must be discreet during their visits."

"I don't think Gnemo got that memo," I said, and Gnedley made a pained face.

"That is another issue entirely," he said.

"Not to be rude, but I have to ask," Marlo burst out. "You look a lot like what we call garden gnomes on our planet. Is that a coincidence? I'm trying to wrap my brain around this."

That was a really good question. Grandpa always said Gnemo looked like a garden gnome, but seeing Gnedley was— well, Marlo was right. Seeing was a whole other experience.

Gnedley had on what I'd call a classic garden gnome getup—pointy red hat, big black boots, and a red shirt. He was about two and a half feet tall, with a little button nose. Very garden gnomelike . . .

If you ignored the big belt with a million pockets, gadgets strapped across his chest, and loads of badges on his shirt. Not to mention the emerald-green skin and dark, curly green hair.

"Although we're supposed to avoid contact," Gnedley said, "incidents still happen." He gestured wryly between the four of us. "The Alliance does their best to remove evidence, but—"

"Sometimes a chatty local tells all their friends?" I supplied.

"Yes," Gnedley admitted. "That's where things get fascinating. You see, when faced with the unexplainable, most individuals prefer an amenable story over the bare truth."

"The Alliance made up garden gnomes stories?" Marlo asked, already shaking her head.

"Quite the opposite," Gnedley said. "Every IC planet we've visited has had their own rich and unique history of folklore. *However*, they've also had one astonishing thing in common. When faced with the unexplainable, they'd adapt a story that made sense. Over time, Alliance sightings have been folded into the mythologies of IC planets across the universe."

"Gnomes taking samples in gardens become garden

gnomes," I said, understanding dawning. It made a strange kind of sense.

"What's the ratio?" Rachel asked.

Gnedley frowned. "What do you mean?"

"What percentage of our myths came from our own stories, and how many came from sloppy crew members?"

Ooh. Excellent question, Rachel. "Yeah," I said. "Are there centaur aliens out there? Or *werewolves*? Or—"

"The percentage of Alliance-driven myths is extremely low," Gnedley said. "Despite contrary evidence, we do keep our leaks to a minimum. Your histories have grown organically, with the occasional Alliance hiccup along the way."

Marlo crossed her arms as she absorbed that, frowning at Gnedley. "Basically, you leave us in the dark to make up explanations until we manage our own methods of deep space travel, all while cheerfully visiting our planet and taking notes?"

"I wouldn't state it quite as simply," Gnedley said. Then he sighed. "But in essence, yes. Attempts at contact were made in the beginning, but crews were lost. The Alliance learned the hard way that an Isolated Community will not adjust before it's ready."

"Oh," Marlo said. "I guess . . . I wasn't really thinking of it from that side."

I had a bad feeling about what crews being lost meant.

From the looks on their faces, so did Marlo and Rachel. The serious turn in the conversation dipped the mood abruptly.

Gnedley toyed with another marshmallow. "What are these made of?"

"Not sure if you want the actual answer to that," I said with a grateful laugh for the change of topic. "Better to just enjoy the deliciousness."

He contemplated that with a hum. "Do you have any—what are they called . . . *hedgehogs*? I would love to see a hedgehog."

"You landed in the wrong spot for that, unfortunately," Marlo said. "They don't live in the wild here."

"Do you ever bring plants and animals from one planet to another?" Rachel slid that in nicely. I did have to admire her stealth skills.

"On *IC planets*?" Gnedley nearly choked on his marshmallow. "Never. That's a huge violation of the code," he said. "Introducing foreign species would have untold consequences for a planet's ecosystem. It's strictly forbidden."

Going by *that* reaction, I didn't think Gnedley was our mushroom farmer.

But did he know who was?

We ate more snacks, chatting while answering Gnedley's questions about Earth. Some of them were straightforward and easy, like "What do humans have against dandelions?"

And others (such as "Why are humans destroying their delicate ecosystems?") required some internet searching and philosophical discussion. The yawns were starting by the time I worked up the courage to ask my big question.

"Gnedley?"

"Mmm?"

"Will you take us to the ship? I need to talk to Gne—Captain Gnemo." If there was even a chance I could convince her to use their medicine to help Grandpa, I was going to take it.

His face fell and he slowly shook his head. "My apologies, Lemon Peabody, but that's impossible." He spoke with a finality I was too familiar with. That tone meant "No, and don't even try to change my mind."

Fine. It would have been easier, but I didn't need Gnedley onboard to make this happen.

"I understand," I said, ignoring a sharp look from Marlo.

Rachel began sharing the wonders of eating marshmallows *and* chocolate with Gnedley as Marlo leaned in close. "What's going on?" she whispered.

"New plan," I whispered back. I held up three fingers. Three words.

Marlo nodded.

Her eyes went round as I mouthed: "Trojan horse Gnedley."

Gnedley

Gnedley left the Humans before the sun rose on 525-1's horizon. They hugged him, offering farewells before returning to their "sleepover," and Gnedley . . .

He needed time to start untangling this mess.

So he walked.

And then walked some more.

Wandering through the woods with his portable shield safely back online, Gnedley reached into his pocket to pull out a small leaf. Identical to Lemon Peabody's.

He'd always viewed IC planets as something to be studied. Analyzed.

Now he realized that although 525-1 might be another file to him—to Lemon Peabody, Marlo García-Reynolds, Rachel

Morris, and Feline Wade . . . it was home.

A home that could be destroyed if he put his trust in the wrong place.

Gnedley had to make his next move carefully. He regretted not being able to fully explain things to the Humans, but he refused to put them in danger. At least, not in any more danger than they'd already placed themselves.

Great Gnominium, he had forgotten to look for the mushrooms! Slumping against a tree, Gnedley tucked the leaf back in his pocket, letting his head fall against the rough bark.

He needed to speak to the commander. Gnedley had a sinking feeling they were coming at things completely wrong. The Gnemo that Lemon described didn't fit with Gnilsson's version.

Yes, she'd broken protocol, but Gnedley now knew how easy it was to cross *that* line.

A mistake made as an ensign was one thing.

Masterminding a criminal empire was another leap entirely.

No. This wasn't right at all.

Gnedley checked his logbook, startling at the time. He'd been in the woods for hours. The others would be wondering where he'd disappeared to. Gnedley hurried to his feet and headed back to the ship. After passing through the barrier, he stopped in surprise. The entire crew sat eating breakfast in front of the loading bay, chuckling as the captain waved one arm through the air.

"Then I said, 'The day I can't tell a sklar weed from a gneet plant is the day I hand in my badge!'" She laughed. "They're probably still trying to get the stains off their ship."

"Sklar weed," Gneelix snorted. "Classic."

Might as well make himself known while everyone was in a good mood. Perhaps he'd skate by on his late return. Gnedley flicked off his shield badge and waved hello. Gnemo, Gneelix, and Gnog stared curiously while Gnilsson leaped up from his crate.

"Ensign." He hurried over, eyebrows speaking volumes. "You're back from *patrol*."

"I am." Gnedley accepted the cover gratefully.

"Did you discover if the Humans obtained any mushrooms?" Gnilsson whispered, pulling him aside as the others resumed their meal.

"I didn't—"

"Then what were you doing?" Gnilsson held his elbow in a crushing grip.

Gnedley yanked it back, and the commander frowned. "I was worried when you didn't return," he said. "I couldn't go and search when I was already covering for your absence."

"I was able to retrieve my logbook," Gnedley said. "But the Humans discovered me."

"You made contact?" Gnilsson inhaled sharply. "Ensign—"

"It was unavoidable," Gnedley whispered, keeping one eye on the crew. "But they knew the Human who met the captain, and the things they told me—Commander, I don't believe Gnemo is involved with this."

"Based on what?" Gnilsson scoffed. "The word of those most likely to be her accomplices?"

"I think—"

"It's not your job to think," Gnilsson snapped. He took a deep breath, his tone softening. "You need to trust that my intel is correct. That I know how to do my job. Do we understand each other?"

Gnedley nodded. He *understood* that Commander Gnilsson had one view of this situation and that nothing Gnedley said would change it.

He understood that he had to solve this on his own.

Gnilsson clapped him on the shoulder and steered them back to the mess area.

"Gnedley," Captain Gnemo said. "If you're done reporting in, have some food and then go to the loading bay. It needs to be sorted if we hope to take off tonight."

"I'll start, Captain," Gnilsson said, heading for the ramp. "It'll be faster with two of us."

"Won't be taking off anywhere if this junker doesn't stop falling apart," Gneelix said, scarfing down the last of her food. "Have better luck building one from scratch." She grabbed her tool bag and stalked off. Gnemo followed at a safe distance.

"You look tired." Doctor Gnog handed Gnedley a plate. "Rough night on patrol?"

"Nothing a bit of . . ." Gnedley dipped a spoon through the sludge on his plate. ". . . breakfast won't fix."

"Undoubtedly." The doctor laughed, picking up their chair to sit in a patch of sun on the other side of the ship.

Gnedley eyed his plate suspiciously. He did not like the sound of that laugh. Scraping the meal into the reprocessing unit, he mentally thanked the Humans for last night's feast, then trotted up the ramp into the hold.

It was a mess. Everything he'd packed was properly labeled and secured, but a large swath of unmarked crates was piled haphazardly in the corner. He peered into the dim recesses of the bay where Gnilsson muttered to himself, making notes in his logbook.

"Commander?"

Gnilsson lurched at Gnedley's voice, nearly knocking over one of the stacks. "Ensign," he said. "I have this well in hand.

I'm sure Gneelix or Gnog could use your assistance."

"But the Capt—"

A jangly noise blasted out from a pocket on Gnedley's belt.

"What's that?" Gnilsson demanded.

"I have no idea." The pocket in question was now vibrating as well. Gnedley carefully opened the flap and withdrew a small blue rectangle. The screen flashed Marlo García-Reynolds's smiling face.

"It would appear you have visitors!" Doctor Gnog called up from the bottom of the ramp.

Gnedley walked out of the hold with trepidation in his hearts.

It couldn't be—

"Gnedley!" A loud bang against the shield made him jump.

He refused to look up. If he didn't see it, it wasn't happening.

"Gnedley, it's us!"

He looked up to see Lemon Peabody outside the barrier with the other two Humans at her side. She waved a small device in her hand, grinning at a spot off to his left. "Answer the phone! Let us in!"

She pointed at Marlo and Rachel, who each brandished a large bag in the air.

"We brought marshmallows!"

CHAPTER 15

Marlo and Rachel had demanded at least *some* sleep after Gnedley had left, a couple of hours earlier. Luckily I was ready to kick off my plan the moment they woke up. Not that I was watching and waiting or anything.

"Stop being creepy, Lemon," Marlo grumbled, rubbing the sleep out of her eyes.

"Not being creepy," I said. "Being ready. Excited to get this show on the road." I'd managed to initiate a group hug before Gnedley had gone so I could slip my phone into one of his many pockets. A definite moment of genius on my part.

"So glad you made us get that friend-stalker app," I said to Marlo as we folded up our sleeping bags.

"Friend Finder," she corrected. "It's for safety, not stalking."

"I'm not about to limit its potential, Marlo."

"What if Gnedley's already discovered your phone and gotten rid of it?" Rachel popped back into the tent after securing her mushroom tote in the shed. "Or what if he doesn't answer?"

Seriously, such optimism with this crew. "Positive thinking, friends! Come on!"

"What if he won't let us in?"

"That, Marlo, is why we need to stop by your kitchen. I know the perfect bribe."

Bribes in hand, we made an appearance at JFR, grabbed our handout from Quinn—"Animal Tracks: When to Follow, When to Run Away"—and beat a fast trail to the clearing. Where I then hollered through the barrier at Gnedley, thumping on the shield as Marlo and Rachel waved their bags of marshmallows . . . to zero response.

"This isn't working," Marlo complained.

"Do not lower that bag," I warned. "Give it a few more minutes." I knocked hard on the barrier. "Gned-*ley*! I know you're in there."

"*What* are you *doing*?" We jumped as he zapped into being beside us.

"Gnedley!" I cried. "Long time no see. We missed you. Can we come in?"

"No!" he said, exasperation flooding his little green face.

"Lemon doesn't really understand that word," Marlo said.

Gnedley frowned, fiddling with the translator on his shirt. "This was working properly."

"No, I meant—never mind. Lemon, you can explain yourself."

"I know you said no, but I don't think I made it clear how much I need to talk to Gnemo." I crouched to look him in the eye. "*Please* let us in."

"The *captain* is the one who sent me to get rid of you," Gnedley huffed, handing over my phone. "Here is your tracking device. You have to leave."

But—

No. That wasn't how this was supposed to go. I shot to my feet and banged on the shield. A sharp buzz punctuated every blow. "Captain Gnemo!" I yelled. "I'm Walt's granddaughter! I have to talk to you, please!" I shook off Marlo's hand and kept banging. "Gnemo! *GNEMO!*"

A device on Gnedley's wrist beeped, and he checked the screen. "She's agreed to let you in," he said, shoulders held stiff. "Join hands and do *not* let go. I'll enter first, and you'll be able to pass behind me." He took my hand, I took Marlo's, and Marlo took Rachel's. Fiddling with a small square device on his belt, he pointed it at the force field, and between one step and the next—

"That's a spaceship," Rachel said in awe.

"Is it though?" Marlo whispered out of the side of her mouth. "I feel like it's missing some pieces."

"This is the *Gnar Five*," Gnedley said proudly. "What do you think?"

In the light of day, it was clear that Saturday night's glimpse hadn't given me the full scope of the ship's . . . everything.

I remembered the sleek oblong spanning the length of the clearing with its two fins. Turned out it wasn't gray, but a mottled green that held echoes of Gnedley's snack moss and definitely didn't scream "Official Vessel of an Intergalactic Organization." A few patch jobs marred the side panels, while a large tear at the rear remained a work in progress. The *Gnar Five* had seen better days.

Gnedley stood to the side, keenly awaiting our reactions.

"It looks *awesome*," I said.

He nodded. "Our most important crew member."

"That she is."

We turned to see four gnomes—Gnomians? Four of Gnedley's shipmates waiting.

The gnome who spoke had silver-streaked sage-colored hair capped off with a perfectly straight pointed blue hat. Sharp eyes took in every detail as they crossed their arms to stare down Gnedley before greeting us with a smile.

"Welcome," the gnome said. "Allow me to make introductions. This is Commander Gnilsson, our first officer." A gnome in a purple shirt stepped forward. They had a good six inches on Gnedley and one of those smiles where it looked like the next words out of their mouth were always going to be "Well, actually . . ."

"He's also our pilot," the first gnome continued, moving down the row. "Doctor Gnog is medic and lab technician. They're the longest-serving Alliance member on our crew." The yellow-outfitted gnome with gray hair tied in a loose braid dipped their head in a serene nod.

The scowl on the next one, dressed in orange, was impressive. "This is Chief Gneelix. She's an engineering wizard." Gneelix tapped a large tool against her leg impatiently, wiping her seafoam-green forehead with a grimy hat.

Which meant—

"And I am Captain Gnemo."

Gnemo.

Grandpa Walt's alien. Right in front of me.

I'd waited years for this moment. Grandpa Walt, even longer. I had to commit every single detail of this moment to memory.

Maybe three feet tall, Gnemo stood ramrod straight, every inch of her holding up the title of Captain. She looked like she could take us down with one hand while eating space moss with the other, and then drive the ship off into the sunset without breaking a sweat.

I think I wanted to be Gnemo when I grew up.

"Ensign Gnedley," she said, words clipped and precise. "Introduce us to your friends."

Gnedley stepped up, wringing his hat between twisting fingers. "Captain, everyone . . . this is Rachel Morris."

Rachel gave a little wave to the crew.

"Marlo García-Reynolds."

Marlo *curtsied*. And instantly glared at me before I could crack a joke.

"And this . . ." Gnedley coughed. "Is Lemon Peabody."

"It's an honor to finally meet you," I said. "Grandpa Walt's told me so much about you. I can't believe you're actually here."

"Walter," Gnemo said softly. "That was a long time ago."

Rachel burst forward before I could respond. "Gneelix!" She blushed and gave a small salute. "Sorry. Um. Chief Gneelix? May I ask you about the algae filtration system?"

"Our ensign's been chatty." Gneelix glared at Gnedley.

Rachel nodded, eyes bright. "He said you designed it yourself and it's one of the most incredible systems in the universe and I would love to hear more about your process and really, *anything* you could possibly tell me would be *amazing*."

"I . . ." Gneelix blinked in surprise and scratched at her ear. "Captain?"

"Have a seat in the mess area, and Chief Gneelix can answer a few questions." Gnemo shot the crew a look. "Within reason."

"Aye, Captain." Gneelix headed over to a group of crates, with Rachel on her heels.

Doctor Gnog offered an arm to Marlo. "Tell me more about these marsh-ma-lows."

Marlo shot me a questioning look, and Gnemo smiled at her. "It's okay," she said. "I would like to speak to your friend for a moment."

I gave her a thumbs-up, and she joined Rachel, followed by Gnilsson and Gnedley—leaving Captain Gnemo and me alone.

"I kind of can't believe you're real," I said, unable to help the laugh that escaped. "Grandpa's talked about you my *whole life*, and here you are."

Every line in her gentled. "How is Walter?"

A simple question with a complicated answer. "He's living it up at the seniors' home these days," I said. "Meeting his daily nap quota. Still believing in aliens." I let my grin fall away as the rest of it reared its ugly head.

"He's getting old." I pushed down thoughts of Grandpa

yelling. Looking lost and confused. "He—he's got this illness. It makes him . . . not the same guy you met, but he's still Walt." I nodded to myself. "He's still awesome."

"It's been many years," Gnemo said, looking out at the ship. "And many light-years between them. Neither of us is the same as we were then."

"Let's go see him," I said, brain working a mile a minute. "Before you leave. Give the two of you a chance to catch up." If Gnemo saw him in person . . .

She shook her head solemnly. "That's not possible."

My heart sank. I couldn't let this chance slip through my fingers. "It wouldn't take long—"

"It's too great a risk," Gnemo said. "As much as I'd like to see Walter, I *cannot* justify venturing into the community. The threat of exposure outweighs my own wants."

"You have your shield thingies so no one can see you," I protested, sure the right angle would make her see reason. "Isn't it worth it for a friend?"

"I'm sorry, Lemon." Gnemo sighed. "It's impossible."

That word.

Impossible.

I had come too far and planned too much for *impossible*. Grandpa needed me to succeed.

Think, Lemon, think. "We'll bring Grandpa to you!"

Gnemo looked doubtful. "I'm not sure that's feasible."

It was better than her don't-see-Walter-at-all plan.

"Don't you want to see him?" I clasped my hands to my chest. "He talks about your visit all the time. Did it only mean something to him?"

"Of course not," Gnemo said firmly. "Meeting Walter . . . understand that I was an ensign at the time, like Gnedley. A young sprout with more confidence than sense. My very first mission, and I flouted the rules for an opportunity to make contact."

"Not that Grandpa was a bad choice for introductions."

"True." She laughed. "It could have been a disaster, but I was lucky Walt was so open-minded. I think he got over his shock faster than I did."

"He's pretty good at rolling with things," I agreed. Or he used to be.

"Looking back," Gnemo said, her smile fading into something more serious, "it seems like more than luck. I think meeting Walt was meant to be. Speaking with your grandfather, sharing our worlds—it dismantled my preconceived notions about IC planets. And at the best possible moment."

"Really?"

Gnemo nodded. "It redirected my entire career," she said. "For the better. Without Walt, I wouldn't have chosen the path of custodianship for these communities. Wouldn't have deemed it a worthy choice."

"Then take the time to thank him!" Why was I the only one seeing sense here?

"Lemon—"

"Forget about rules," I said. "Do you want to leave knowing you could have seen him and you *didn't*? That this friend you haven't seen in *thirty years*, who helped change your life, wasn't even worth a *hello*?"

Captain Gnemo slid a hand down her face, shooting me a flat look. "We take off in ten Earth hours. We will not wait for you."

I did the math quickly in my head. Takeoff at eight p.m. No problem. I could have Grandpa in for a visit and back to the home without anyone the wiser.

"We'll be here," I promised.

I'd tackle asking her to help Grandpa when we came back. Once they were face-to-face again, there was no way Gnemo could refuse.

At least I hoped so.

She called the other gnomes back, and Marlo smiled at Gnedley as we said our good-byes. "It was really cool to meet you," she said. "I think I'll name my next character after you."

Gnedley beamed while my jaw hit the ground. What's a girl

got to do to be immortalized in her best friend's literature?

She's going to worry about it later, because this girl's on a deadline.

"I'm gonna make it happen," I said to Gnemo before we disappeared through the shield.

Marlo tilted her head curiously but kept quiet until we'd moved away from the clearing. "What was that about?" she asked.

"Gnemo won't come see Grandpa," I said. "But I've got a few hours to figure it out."

"Figure what out?" Marlo said, sensors already set to wary.

"How to get Walt out through his window."

Gnedley

Gnedley returned from escorting the Humans through the barrier to find the captain waiting.

"Ensign," she said. "Walk with me."

He fell into step beside her as the rest of the crew entered the ship, allowing them a modicum of privacy.

"You engaged with the inhabitants of an IC planet," she began. "Allowed yourself to be compromised and revealed our ship's location. You breached countless protocols—"

"So did *you*," Gnedley snapped. He stopped short, shocked by the vehemence of his anger, but there was no stopping the torrent of words. "Those Humans had been wandering the woods for days. Looking for *you*. Because of *your* breach of protocol. All of this happened *because* of *you*."

As the anger spilled out, the hurt crept in.

"You drilled me on the handbook. Limited the range of my patrol—"

Gnemo cocked her head. "I didn't—"

"I tried my best to live up to your standards," Gnedley said. "But it was all a lie."

The captain nodded, silently absorbing his words. "When you joined the crew," she said, "I saw so much of my younger self in you." Gnemo smiled faintly. "I thought leading by strict example was the best way to keep you on the right path, but now I realize that was a mistake. Honesty would have served us better."

She took a deep breath and faced him straight on. "When I was an ensign, I came across a Human on patrol. I let curiosity get the better of me and spoke with him. It was . . ." Gnemo shook her head with a laugh. "One of the best nights of my life."

Gnedley knew the feeling.

"But I was lucky," she said. "That Human could have tried to capture or harm me. I could have been used to expose the Alliance to the entire planet."

Gnedley swallowed hard. He'd been lucky in that respect too.

"I was also fortunate to have a captain who gave me a second chance instead of a discharge," she continued, eyeing him meaningfully. "I'm going to tell you what they told me."

He nodded, grateful beyond words that he wasn't about to be discharged either. Gnemo laid a hand on his shoulder and looked him in the eye.

"Every member of the Alliance has been in your boots," she said. "Curiosity is a powerful, wondrous thing. It's why we're all here. The Alliance is a celebration of curiosity." Gnemo pointed to the woods beyond the shield. "But now you're learning what it is to *be* a member of the Alliance. How visiting an Isolated Community means one wrong move can change the course of an entire planet. It's a heavy responsibility, Gnedley."

Captain Gnemo looked back at him. "With this second chance," she said, "you have to decide if you can bear it."

Could he? Travel to these planets and always keep a step apart?

After his experience with the Humans, Gnedley wasn't sure.

But he couldn't imagine *never* traveling to an IC planet ever again. Not when there was so much to learn. "I—I think I can," he said, trying to feel convinced of that.

Gnemo watched him carefully. "Sleep on it," she said. "After we've managed to take off tonight, and then we'll talk again tomorrow."

She led him back to the ship, and they joined the crew in launch prep.

In a few hours, they'd be leaving 525-1 behind.

Gnedley hoped sleeping on it would help him feel better about that fact.

CHAPTER 16

Marlo and Rachel were not fans of the new plan.

"No," Marlo said, stomping her foot. "I'm literally putting my foot down. You can't actually think this will work."

I paced back and forth between the trees. We hadn't even made it out of the woods before the two of them mutinied. "You're bringing a lot of negative energy here, Marlo."

"Your grandpa is, what, seventy-five?" she snapped. "He's already got one bad hip. You try sneaking him out the window, he's gonna break the other one."

"The window thing has flaws," I conceded. "Maybe with a distraction, we could take him out a side door." Sully would help with that.

"The method is only half the problem," Rachel cut in.

"We're still kidnapping a senior citizen and leading him into the woods. I didn't sign up for that."

"It's Grandpa," I said. "Not a random senior citizen."

"Who could fall and get hurt, or disoriented, or overwhelmed." Rachel listed off the minuses like the least helpful team member ever. "The home could call your parents or the police. How do you think that'll end, Lemon?"

"But I need—"

"It's not all about *you*." Rachel's sharp voice cut down to the meat of it. "I'm not putting myself in that situation." She leveled a look at Marlo. "Don't know why you would either."

"My parents *would* actually freak out," Marlo said, frowning to herself.

"The mushrooms." I snapped my fingers. "It's your last chance to ask the gnomes about them and get answers."

"I can't. You heard Gnedley," Rachel countered, shoving her glasses up with one finger. "I'm not giving them an open invitation to confiscate my only samples."

"Then why are you here?" I burst out, frustration bubbling over. "Why don't you take your stupid mushrooms and leave? I'll figure this out on my own."

"Fine. Good idea." Rachel grabbed her bag.

"Lemon," Marlo scolded me softly. "Rachel, wait."

She stopped, arms hugged tight against her sides, before

spinning around to face us. "No," she said. "We were going to be a team, and *this* is not a team. I don't know what your deal is, Lemon, but you're being a jerk. I'm going home."

She walked away without looking back, and Marlo made an exasperated noise.

"What is *wrong* with you?"

With me? What about my supposed friends?

"You can go too." I shrugged. "I'm done arguing. I've got things to do."

"Are you serious?" She threw her hands in the air. "I've done nothing but help, and you're giving me attitude?"

"You obviously *don't* want to help anymore, so I'll do this myself."

I didn't need Rachel and I didn't need Marlo.

Just me and Grandpa, like it's been from the beginning.

I whipped through our front door and chucked my bag on the floor.

"Lemon?"

I froze at my dad's voice. That wasn't right.

"What are you doing home?" we asked at the same time.

I found him in the kitchen, standing in front of a pile of stuff on the table, blocking it from view. "Junior Forest Rangers let out early," I said. "Why are you here?" A familiar binder at the bottom of the pile caught my eye. "Is that—"

I ducked under Dad's arm and pawed through the pile. Star charts. Notes. Log printouts.

Every single thing from Project Validation.

"Why is this here?" All of our hard work. Thrown on the kitchen table. It looked jarringly out of place. It should be tucked safely away at Grandpa's, ready for notes on our new findings.

"I cleared your alien stuff out of Walter's place," Dad said, like it was normal. Like a trip to the grocery store. Like "Hey, Lemon, I picked up cereal and violated your Grandpa's privacy on the way home."

"I can *see* that." I pulled out the binder and gripped it to my chest. "*Why?* You had no right to take any of this."

"Your grandfather didn't know where half this stuff was." Dad flicked a page. "Frankly, he won't remember it's gone. This is for the best."

"Says who?" Why did he get to judge?

"I've seen how excited you've been this week," he said. "Moving on to other activities has been good for you."

"You *made me*." I snapped back. "The *only* reason—" My mouth slammed shut. I couldn't tell him that my excitement had nothing to do with Junior Forest Rangers.

I didn't *want* to tell him.

He didn't deserve to know.

Dad could find out later and realize how wrong he'd been. Holding the binder in one arm, I scooped as much of the rest of it off the table as I could carry. "This doesn't belong to you."

"Lenore," he said, pinching the bridge of his nose with a huff.

"Don't throw the rest out," I warned, heading to my room. "I'm coming back."

I managed it in two trips, without speaking a word to Dad. Mom got home shortly after that, and their hushed voices drifted up the stairs. I skipped dinner and holed up in my room. As much as I wanted to break Grandpa out now, I had to wait.

Fewer staff in the evening meant fewer eyes.

By seven p.m., dusk had settled and it was quiet outside. Time to go.

I headed downstairs, and my parents emerged from the kitchen as I slipped my shoes on. "Going for a walk," I said. "Is that an acceptable activity?"

"Sweetie," Mom said. "We should talk."

"I don't think I can right now." It wasn't even a lie. "Things'll go better if I get some air and clear my head."

She and Dad exchanged a look before nodding. "Don't go far," she said. "Back in half an hour, and take your phone."

I waved it at her before stuffing it in my pocket on the way out. That curfew could be pushed with a few well-timed texts. Nothing was stopping me from getting Grandpa to Gnemo.

I wasn't an idiot. This could go wrong a thousand different ways, but how could I live with myself if I didn't even try?

The front entrance of Shady Elms was quiet, but I wasn't taking any chances. I boosted myself up to Grandpa's window and exhaled in relief. Unlocked. Sliding back the screen, I squeezed through and tiptoed into the room. The clock might be ticking, but I couldn't afford to draw any attention.

Grandpa Walt snoozed in his chair. Reading lamp still on. Surprise, surprise. His face was slack as he snored softly, glasses slipping down his nose.

"Grandpa, wake up," I whispered.

He mumbled and I gently shook his shoulder. "Grandpa!"

"Wha—? What?" Grandpa woke with a gasp, pitching forward and sending his glasses flying. He hazily searched the room before stopping on me, and he frowned. "Who's there?" he asked, voice rising. "What are you doing in my room?"

"It's okay, it's me." Right, he couldn't see without his glasses. I reached down and handed them over. "Here."

Grandpa slid them on with a shaky hand. "What do you want?"

Wait.

"Grandpa," I leaned closer and he reared back. "It's me."

"Who?" He looked confused and a little bit scared and I realized . . .

He didn't recognize me.

He didn't know who I was.

No.

Not now.

Not yet.

"Grandpa, it's *me*," I said, my throat going tight. "Lemon. I'm Lemon."

He stared, and I thought, You can't leave when we're so close.

"Lemon?" Grandpa Walt blinked, adjusting his glasses. "W-what's going on?"

"Grandpa, it's Gnemo." I crouched beside his chair. "I found her. We need to go."

"No, no," Grandpa rubbed at his forehead. "I don't feel well. I can't."

"Come on, Grandpa. Don't give up on me now."

Someone knocked, but I ignored it.

"Grandpa, Project Validation." I tried to coax him up. "You can do it. Let's go."

"Stop," Grandpa shouted, pulling his hand from mine. "Stop!"

It felt like a slap.

"Stop bothering me. I'm tired." He sank back against his chair, still halfway yelling. "Leave me alone."

"Grandpa—"

"Leave me *alone*!"

The door opened and Nurse Edie rushed in, speaking in low tones. "It's okay, Lemon, let me handle this."

A soft, warm hand pressed into my shoulder, leading me out into the hall.

"Here now, Lemon-ade." Sully.

He tucked a tissue into my hand. I stared at it until he picked it back up, pressing lightly against my wet cheeks. "It'll be all right, sweetheart."

No. I shook my head fiercely. It really wouldn't.

Sully tucked me into his side and we stood like that, together, as Grandpa's shouts echoed down the hall.

CHAPTER 17

Mom and Dad showed up soon after that.

Dad disappeared into Grandpa's room and Mom thanked Sully for his help.

Dad came back and ushered us to the car.

We drove home.

I followed Mom and Dad into the house and on to the kitchen.

Dad at least waited until Mom and I sat down before letting loose.

"What were you thinking?" he yelled, pacing in front of the cupboards. "Taking your grandfather? To hunt aliens in the woods? I don't know. . . . What can I say to get through to you? You *can't keep doing this*."

"Patrick—"

"No, Olivia, she needs to hear it," he said. "I was younger than her when I accepted the truth. She's past due."

I knew where this was headed. My hands curled into fists under the table, but he kept going before I could speak.

Patrick Peabody had something to say, and no one was going to stop him.

"There are no aliens." Dad carefully enunciated every word. "I know it. You know it. Your grandfather knows it. The difference is, I can admit it. They never existed."

"You sure about that?" A tiny, slightly hysterical giggle slipped out at the thought of Gnemo and her ship, waiting. "Super sure?"

"This is what I mean," Dad said to Mom. "She's impossible. I should have put a stop to this years ago." His voice inched up into a harsher note. "He *lied*, Lenore. His story is fake."

I couldn't listen to this. "It's not!" I shouted back. "It's all true."

Mom turned in her seat, wrapping an arm around my shoulder. "Sometimes people get attached to a story—"

"It's *not* just a story, Mom."

"I think we should be discussing what happened in there," she said. "Can you tell us what Grandpa said? Why he got so upset?"

Grandpa's face flashed in my mind. Him saying "Who?"

"He didn't recognize me," I whispered. "It was just for a second, but . . . he was upset."

"Oh, sweetheart." She brought me in for a tight hug.

"This is why we had a routine in place." Dad scrubbed a hand down his face.

"So if I went every day at three p.m., this wouldn't have happened?" I threw my hands up. "If I only talk about approved topics, he won't forget me again? Is that how this works?"

"You know that's not what I mean," he said, dropping heavily into a chair on the other side of Mom.

"You have all of these rules!" I cried. "But it feels like I'm the only one who wants to help him get better."

"There's no cure for Alzheimer's, honey." Mom said gently. "We've talked about this. There's no fix. It's going to be hard, but your dad and I are here for you. And for Grandpa. To help him the best we can."

I couldn't help it. I laughed.

"Dad doesn't want to help Grandpa," I said bitterly.

Dad looked at me, face carefully blank.

If we were talking about this . . . we were really going to talk about it.

Now *I* had something to say.

"I think part of you is happy he's losing his memory," I

spat. "Happy he'll forget the aliens. Forget his story. You've always hated it."

"He's going to forget *us* before he forgets his damn story." Dad stood, hands shaking.

My breath caught in my chest as each word struck home.

I wanted to yell back. Tell him to shut up. To stop *lying*.

But I couldn't speak. Could barely breathe.

"Do you understand?" Dad's shout roughly faded away. "He's going to keep losing himself, bit by bit. Eventually Grandpa won't be the man we remember." He shook his head. "I don't know how you could think I'd ever be *happy* about that."

I stared at the table, blinking back tears.

I didn't want to talk about this anymore. Didn't want to think about it.

Because I *was* starting to understand.

Mom cleared her throat. "I think it's been a difficult night, and sleep would be the best thing for everyone," she said. "We can talk more in the morning. Is anyone hungry?"

My stomach rolled at the thought of eating. "I'm going to bed," I mumbled, escaping the kitchen for my room.

Shutting the door carefully behind me, I flung myself onto my bed and closed my eyes against the memories of the last few hours.

Rachel and Marlo's hurt. Grandpa's confusion. Dad's anger.

I'd made a huge mess of things.

My phone alarm beeped. Eight p.m.

Gnemo was gone, taking any hope I had of helping Grandpa with her.

Later that night, I crept onto the landing for a drink of water from the bathroom. Voices from my parents' bedroom froze me in place. Hopefully they hadn't heard the creaking floor.

"You need to talk to her," Mom said. "How can she understand if you don't explain where you're coming from?"

Dad sighed. "She idolizes my dad. Always has. Nothing I say will get through. I'm the bad guy who doesn't believe."

And he hasn't. Not since I could remember.

"She'll never know why unless you tell her," Mom insisted softly. "You can't just yell. Share how you feel. What you went through with your dad."

"What's the point?" Dad asked. "It's too late. It's—"

"Don't do that," Mom said. "You don't get to give up when I'm here trying to help you through it."

It was silent long enough I thought they'd gone to sleep, but then Dad took a shaky breath. "I wish . . . I wanted to protect her," he said. "Save her from the Walter Peabody bandwagon. I know where that goes, and I didn't want her getting her heart broken."

"Then maybe," Mom said, "you should stop being the one to do it. Talk to her, Patrick. I mean it."

Their voices faded to a murmur and I crept back to my room, more confused than ever.

Gnedley

The *Gnar Five* was going nowhere.

A truly terrible sound emerged when Gneelix had fired up the drives.

She did not take it well.

After a fitful attempt at sleep, Gnedley was brooding in his bunk, reviewing the chaos of the day. Between the visit from the Humans, his discussion with Gnemo, and multiple disasters with the launch attempt, he'd had no time for further investigation of the mushroom situation.

Every instinct said he should come clean to the captain. Commander Gnilsson might disagree, but Gnedley couldn't keep lying to her. Not after her own honesty today.

Tomorrow he would lay it all out for her.

But first—

There was one detail that kept needling at him. Something he knew he had to check if he was going to bring Gnemo all the pieces of this puzzle.

The extra crates.

Gnedley rolled out of bed and tossed on his uniform. Tiptoeing through the ship, he made his way to the hold. Everything was tidied up, but he knew what he was looking for.

He headed to the back corner where the crates Commander Gnilsson had been working on were now labeled and secured. Gnedley carefully cracked open the lid of the closest crate. If it was "soil samples," as listed, he could pack it back up, worries abated.

It was not soil samples.

He raked his eyes over the rows of meticulously packed, glowing mushrooms.

By regulations, they should have been destroyed. Or neutralized and packed up as evidence. Not . . . stored and prepped as though ready for sale . . .

"I wish you hadn't done that, Ensign."

Gnedley whirled around, dropping the lid to the floor.

Commander Gnilsson watched him with a calculating gaze. "What are the chances of you walking away?"

The puzzle pieces fell into place with a sickening thud. It

had been the commander all along. And Gnedley had *trusted* him. He was a foolish sprout indeed. Gnedley swallowed hard against the shame rising in his throat.

There was still time.

He could make things right.

"I have to tell the captain." Gnedley shook his head. "I can't—"

"Of course you can," Gnilsson said. "Once I have all the mushrooms, my buyers will arrive, and I'll leave with them." He smiled genially. "You and the crew will be free to finish your repairs and leave. Everyone's happy."

The commander moved to block Gnedley's path of escape. "Run and tell Gnemo if you wish," he said. "But I'll be forced to tell her how I found you at the mushroom patch and realized why you keep disappearing on patrol."

Dread crept up Gnedley's spine as he began to see how Gnilsson had engineered his part in this mess. "Because you *asked* me to—"

"Your word against mine. What do you think she'll say when I tell her that I discovered your codes were used to access our system and take down the comms? How shocked I was when I realized your plan and how I've been trying *so hard* to help you find a way out of this misguided scheme . . ."

"Why are you doing this?" Gnedley whispered.

"I saw an opportunity and I took it." Gnilsson shrugged. "And I'm nearly there—except your Humans still have some of my stock."

His Humans?

"I would like you to retrieve it," the commander said. "Tonight."

Gnedley scowled. He wasn't bringing the Humans back into this if he could help it. "I think I'll take my chances with the captain instead."

"I'll ask them myself then." Gnilsson pulled a laser pruner off his belt. He flicked it on and idly cut a slice through the crate lid on the floor. "I can be persuasive."

"Fine," Gnedley bit out, the betrayal burning in his gut. "I'll get them."

"Good choice, sprout." He ducked as Gnilsson reached to ruffle his hair and then headed for the ramp, settling his hat firmly upon his head.

Good choice?

No choice.

Gnedley silently pulled open the door to the small structure in Marlo García-Reynolds's yard. It was where he'd spent the most time with the Humans and he was hoping they might have entrusted it with their stash of mushrooms. He searched the darkened room.

Mostly rustic tools and insect carcasses until—

There. A medium-sized box sat tucked under the rickety table. Gnedley tugged it out, lifted the lid, and stewed at the large cluster of mushrooms carefully packed in the bottom.

He'd hoped they hadn't stumbled upon the mushrooms, but at least now he could put a stop to any further involvement. Confiscating the fungi was for their own good. Commander Gnilsson wouldn't be the worst individual hunting for such a treasure trove.

Gnedley hefted the box into his arms. It felt heavier than it should, weighted down with his own foolishness. He cursed himself for believing Gnilsson's manipulations.

He'd been deceived from the start.

Heading back for the ship, he set a slow pace. He could use the time to figure out how to make it right.

CHAPTER 18

Soft light filtered through my blinds, poking past my eyelids, and I groaned. How dare the world keep spinning after yesterday's disaster?

I flipped the blanket over my head.

My bedroom door clicked open. "Sweetie," Mom whispered as she came up beside my bed. "Dad and I are going to work."

She pulled back the blanket, gently brushing the hair from my face, and I kept my eyes screwed shut. She knew I was awake, but that didn't mean I was ready to chat.

"Remember the rules of your grounding," she said. "No leaving the house, no internet, no phone unless it's an emergency." An expectant pause. "Lemon."

"Understood." I slipped a hand out from under the

covers and gave her a thumbs-up. "The outside world is but a memory."

Mom grabbed my hand, unfurling my fingers to thread hers in between. "Call Sofía if you need anything. Your dad will be home at lunch to check on you."

I cracked an eye open to give her a Look.

"Listen." She squeezed my hand. "Last night was hard, but I think talking was a good start and we should do more of that."

"More of the yelling?" I sank into my pillow.

"More sharing about how we're feeling," she said with a shake of her head and a little smile. "Your dad included. We'll work on it. I promise."

I tried to hide my grimace.

"Speaking of working on things—" Mom tweaked my nose. "I left you a list of chores. Don't stay in bed all day."

"Yup." I offered another thumbs-up.

She blew a kiss over her shoulder on the way out. "Love you."

"Love you too." I burrowed under the blankets, pulling the pillow over my head. It didn't take long for reality to set back in.

Why bother with chores when I'd already ruined everything?

✳ ✳ ✳

"Lemon."

Hands. Shoving me.

"Wake up."

I blinked sleep out of my eyes until a looming Marlo came into focus. "Wha?"

"I can't believe you made me go to Junior Forest Rangers alone," she said.

"Grounded," I grunted.

"I know," she said. "Mama told me what happened and said I could come check on you at first break. Your mom gave me a key." She paused with a smirk. "A *key* is an object people use to go through doors instead of climbing in windows."

"Oh."

Marlo frowned. "Now you say, 'Keys are boring, Marlo.'"

But I couldn't play along. My whole body felt heavy. I wanted to let it sink into my bed and turn off my brain. Stop thinking about how I had failed. How I had disappointed everyone.

A tear squeezed out and slid down my cheek.

"All right, shove over, you big lump." Marlo poked until I created space for her to slide in. She rested her head on the pillow, prodding at my feet with cold toes.

We lay quietly, hearts beating together. Marlo stayed silent until I met her eyes.

"Hey," she whispered. "Talk to me."

I wanted to say "I'm sorry."

Sorry for pulling you along on one bad plan after another.

Sorry I didn't listen to you.

What came out was . . .

"My grandpa's sick."

Marlo nodded, and I swallowed thickly.

"He's not going to get better," I said, voice cracking.

"That really sucks," she said.

"I wanted to help, but it wasn't enough." Swiping furiously at my eyes wasn't cutting it. I pressed my palms into them instead. "Ugh, so stupid."

"Tell me," Marlo said softly.

"Gnedley fixed Rachel's arm with that worm bandage in . . . in *seconds*, you know? And I thought, maybe . . . if I could bring Gnemo and Grandpa together, she could . . ."

I had to take a breath.

"She could cure him."

I groaned at Marlo's sigh. "I know," I said. "At first, all I wanted was to find them, but then—I got the idea in my head and I couldn't stop. Like I said, stupid."

"Stop with the stupid." Marlo pulled my hands away from my face. "Pretty sure that language is banned in our friendship contract."

I snorted. She wasn't wrong.

"I get why you thought that," she said.

"Really?" I shuffled up to look at her properly.

"Yes! Aliens?" Marlo laughed. "Kinda opens up a whole new world of possibilities."

Glad I wasn't the only one who'd had their mind blown.

"I get it," she said. "Why you wanted to try."

"You do?"

"Remember when my abuelo died?" Marlo asked.

How could I forget? When he'd passed away from a stroke two years ago, we'd all been in shock. Marlo's abuelo was awesome. He only managed the trip a couple of times a year, but he'd visit for weeks at a time. When we were little, he danced us around on his feet, and he always teased Marlo about life giving her lemons.

"I remember," I whispered.

"I was so *mad*," Marlo said, wiping away her own tears. "I didn't get to say goodbye. He was just gone. With your grandpa . . ." She reached for my hand as she spoke. "I realized it could go the other way."

"It's like a new goodbye every time." My voice broke a bit, and she squeezed my hand tight. Holding me in place. "I feel like he's dying a little bit every day," I said. "And one day, his body's going to be here. But *he's* not."

"I know." Marlo nodded, and that was it.

I started to cry and I couldn't stop. I'd said it. Said the worst thing out loud and now—

I couldn't ignore it.

Marlo cried with me. And weirdly enough, having someone to cry with made it easier to let it out.

Eventually the tears stopped, and I took a shuddery breath.

Marlo patted my face with a corner of the blanket. "This is so not hygienic, but I have no idea where the tissues are in this disaster you call a room." She laughed as she did a quick swipe under her own eyes. "How ya doing?"

"I don't know what I was thinking," I said. "Dad wouldn't believe me if I shoved an alien in his face and I—I think I made Grandpa worse."

"No," Marlo said fiercely. "I've seen your Grandpa's face when you're working on Project Validation together. It makes him so happy. That's what matters. Although I'm sure shoving an alien in your dad's face would've been awesome."

"So awesome," I agreed, probably a little too wholeheartedly.

She laughed before settling back into a serious stare. "I did some reading with my moms about Alzheimer's. Your grandpa is getting worse, but . . ." She poked me until I met her eyes again. "Not because of you. It's how his condition works."

"I know that *here*." I pointed to my head. "It's hard to know it here," I said, moving my hand to my heart. "Not like it matters. Gnemo's gone."

"We don't know if they could have done anything," Marlo said.

The problem in a nutshell. "And now we'll never know."

"I think you need to talk to your mom and dad," she said, and I scoffed.

"Because that's gone great so far."

She leveled a glare at me. "Have you told them what you're worried about?"

"Not everyone's parents talk about things as easily as yours do," I said. "My mom's trying, but . . ."

We sank back into the pillow. Marlo's hand found mine again and gave it a squeeze.

"I'm sorry," I said, getting to what I *should* have said when she arrived. "For being such a jerk and dragging you into this mess."

"I'm pretty used to being dragged into your messes," Marlo said. "But you were definitely a jerk, so apology appreciated and accepted." She snuggled in. "You know who else you owe one to . . ."

"Rachel," I groaned. "I was so nasty to her. She probably hates me."

Marlo's phone beeped, and she checked the screen after it went off three more times in a row. "It's her," Marlo reported. "She's freaking out. The shield's gone from the patch and someone cleared out the mushrooms!" She scrolled through the messages. "Rachel managed to find a hidden clump, and she wants to pick up the tote she left at my place."

I checked the time. "I could go and make it back before Dad's home for lunch," I said, scrambling off the bed.

At least I had a hope at fixing one more of my mistakes today.

CHAPTER 19

Rachel was waiting by Marlo's backyard gate when we arrived, a small box clutched in her hands.

"Thanks for coming," she said to Marlo. "I would've stopped by yesterday, but—" She cut a glance my way.

She didn't want to risk running into me. Way to alienate your new friend, Lemon.

Heh. Alienate.

Stop it. Get serious. You're here to apologize.

"At first I worried about leaving them in the tote," Rachel said. "But they appear to thrive in any habitat. Cultivating them should be easy compared to mycorrhizal fungi—"

"Mycor-what?" I blurted out.

"Mycorrhizal," Rachel answered stiffly. "It's fungus that

requires a symbiotic relationship with other plants to thrive." She paused, adding with a bit of snark, "Symbiotic means mutually beneficial."

"Which our friendship wasn't," I said. "I owe you an apology."

"Yes, you do," she agreed.

I stopped myself from stepping forward. She held the box up like a shield, body language screaming she wouldn't be okay with a hug-it-out apology like Marlo. "I'm sorry for how I treated you and the things I said." I took a deep breath, hoping she felt the truth of my words. "I was rude and mean and that's not the kind of friend I want to be."

"And?"

"And I'm sorry I was selfish and focused on my own problems and didn't help with the mushrooms like I promised I would."

"Apology accepted," Rachel said.

That was . . . a bigger relief than I expected it to be.

It felt right having her back with us.

"On one condition," she continued, holding up a finger. "Tell me what time you left the gnomes last night. Do you know when they took off? We need a timeline. I'm concerned about how many other people may have come across the leftover mushrooms."

"Uh—"

"Did the gnomes mention anything?" Rachel asked. "We can't rule out the possibility that the shield glitched and someone else cleared the patch."

"Grandpa and I . . . he couldn't . . . we didn't go back. I didn't get to see the gnomes before they left, so I don't know when they did this. Or if they did. Or didn't." I honestly wasn't sure what the question was anymore.

Understanding dawned in Rachel's eyes. "I'm sorry it didn't work out."

I nodded my thanks. I was too.

"Glad we got that sorted and we're all friends again." Marlo swung the fence door open. "Come on, your mushrooms are still in the shed. We've got to get Lemon home before she turns into a pumpkin."

We trooped across the backyard and Wade chirped as he appeared, quickly ducking my attempts to pet him. Classic Wade.

Marlo flipped on the shed light to reveal . . .

No tote box.

"I swear we left it right here." She crouched to look under the table.

I checked behind the door, still halfway open. Nothing.

"Who would take them?" No one but the three of us knew

they were there. "Marlo, did your moms come out here at all?"

"No!" she exclaimed, dusting the dirt off her hands. "I don't get it."

"Gnedley," Rachel said, defeated. "We *thought* one of the gnomes was behind the patch. He probably spotted the tote on Wednesday and came back for it."

"I had no choice." Gnedley appeared out of nowhere, and the three of us shrieked.

"Don't *do* that!" I yelled.

"My apologies, Lemon Peabody, but things have become far too dire for niceties."

"Explain," Rachel demanded. Mess with her science, she'll make you answer for it.

"Commander Gnilsson is behind the crop," Gnedley said. "He threatened physical harm against you unless I retrieved the mushrooms in your possession."

"Whoa," Marlo said, and Gnedley nodded.

"He is single-minded in his goal. I learned he placed invisible biotrackers on you during your visit to the ship."

Wait, what? I caught Marlo trying to peek at her back over her shoulder as I surreptitiously checked under my arm.

"During the handshake," Rachel exclaimed, and we all looked at our hands in dismay.

"The trackers are immaterial. They'll dissipate in a few

days." Gnedley tore off his hat, scratching a hand through his curls. "When I returned with your box, the commander was incensed. He'd spotted one of you on his map, visiting the site."

Marlo and I did our best *not* to look in Rachel's direction.

"I convinced him to let me do a final sweep to ensure there were no mushrooms left in your possession," Gnedley said. "So I could warn you—don't go back. It's too dangerous."

"What's going on?" None of this made sense. "Why haven't you left yet?"

"Gnilsson sabotaged the ship." Gnedley's face turned murderous. "I suspect he caused our near-crash, and now he has *pirates* coming to buy his illegal goods."

"Pirates!" I wheezed.

"Illegal?" Marlo gulped.

"Those are no mere mushrooms," Gnedley said darkly.

"I knew it," Rachel whispered, shoving the box into Marlo's hands before grabbing her phone from her pocket. "Tell me *everything*."

"That is highly classified information." Gnedley shook his head. "The fungi's presence alone puts you all in grave danger."

Marlo and I froze. Wade took the opportunity to weave between Marlo's legs, purring loudly despite the tension.

"Uh, what?" Any other rational response to that news flew out of my head.

"I'm not giving them up," Rachel said stubbornly.

"You must—believe me, they're more powerful than you could imagine," Gnedley said. "Members of the Alliance have died trying to contain them."

"Died?" Marlo squeaked. She dropped the box, and mushrooms spilled out onto the floor.

"Marlo!" Rachel yelled.

Wade crept up, stalking the ones rolling at our feet. Panic laced Gnedley's voice as he shouted at him to stop, but it was too late. None of us were able to move fast enough to catch Wade mid-pounce, and he landed on the closest mushroom.

Between one breath and the next, it exploded in a bright shower of sparks, taking Wade along with it.

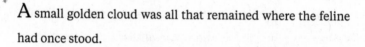

Gnedley

A small golden cloud was all that remained where the feline had once stood.

"*Wade?*" Marlo cried.

The device in Rachel's hand clicked.

"My cat just *died*," Marlo said, turning to her. "And you take a *picture*?"

Oh, Great Gnominium. He had to get this situation under control. "Marlo," he said, touching the weeping Human's arm. "Your cat is not dead."

"W-what?" She blinked through watery eyes.

"Are you sure?" Lemon asked, pinching her nose. "Because, no offense, but it kinda smells like it."

The golden cloud meowed faintly.

"Wade?" Marlo whispered.

"The same color as the bioluminescence," Rachel muttered, tapping on her device.

"Gnedley," Lemon said. "Would you please explain what all of that was?" She waved a hand through the air, which Gnedley would have advised against. "Oh, no," she gagged. "Nobody move. It makes it worse."

Gnedley sighed. He'd hoped to avoid sharing this information so the Humans could plead ignorance if anyone came calling. Knowing meant no going back.

"Tell me what's happening," Marlo demanded, clutching Lemon, who nodded fiercely.

So be it.

"This fungi is known for the gas it produces," he said, pointing to the cloud. "When it's released, the gas combines with the spores to form a golden mist."

"And stench," Lemon added.

"And a very distinctive odor," Gnedley acknowledged. "If the mist releases around a being, the spores will stick, and eventually, recombine with the gas—"

They looked to the cloud, which was beginning to dissipate, leaving an empty space.

"—to render the being invisible."

"Wade?" Marlo stroked the air with a shaky hand,

and a rumbly purr filled the room.

"It wears off after approximately two Earth hours," Gnedley assured her. "Less for Feline Wade, since these mushrooms are not yet at full maturation."

Unlike the dozens of full crates Commander Gnilsson had on board.

"How does it work?" Rachel asked, eyeing the remaining fungi on the floor.

"That was *clearly* magic," Lemon chimed in.

Rachel frowned, pushing her glasses up her nose. "Not knowing how it works doesn't mean it's magic."

Gnedley agreed with the sentiment, however—

"It *is* a little mystifying," he said. "Scientists across the universe have attempted to discern the exact process that occurs, but there's no clear-cut explanation."

"That means they have no idea," Marlo whispered to Lemon, who tapped the side of her head sagely.

"Best hypothesis?" Rachel picked up a mushroom and the other Humans followed suit, turning them over to watch the faint glow.

"The chemical combination of the gas and the spores appears to bend the light." Gnedley pointed at the floor. "Look closely and you'll see Wade is not entirely invisible."

The Humans peered at the space. There was a slight blur,

as though catching sight of something from the corner of your eye.

"But he'll definitely be okay?" Marlo watched the blur nervously.

"Most definitely." To the best of his knowledge, the creatures of IC 525-1 had never been exposed to the gas, but Gnedley felt confident there would be no ill effects.

Hopefully.

"At least the stink is wearing off," Lemon muttered.

The door creaked open as Wade slipped outside. "He's gonna have a field day," Marlo said, staring after him. "RIP neighborhood birds."

"What exactly is the gas?" Rachel asked. "The components?"

"Ah." Gnedley hemmed and hawed. "That's the other mystifying part."

"Again I say *magic*! This is amazing," Lemon said. "What could be dangerous about a magic mushroom that turns you invisible?" She paused, taking a breath. "Okay, as I said it, I had some ideas why, but I still want to know."

Since, as the Humans liked to say, the cat was out of the bag . . . and invisible, Gnedley realized they might be more inclined to cooperate if they understood the full history of their find.

"The fungi's common name is thieves' gold," he said. "It's well loved by criminals across the universe. The spore cloud masks body temperature. A cloaking shield can be detected as can other technology, but thieves' gold is untraceable."

"Aside from the smell," Lemon interjected.

"They thrive in nearly every atmosphere," Gnedley pressed on. "And the growth cycle allows for rapid disbursement. A single fruit body can set up a criminal *empire*. If left unchecked . . . as an Alliance member, I'm duty bound to destroy them."

"You can't." Rachel curled her hands around the mushroom. "I have to study—"

"This concerns not only your safety, but your entire planet's," Gnedley said, hoping to make her understand. "If smugglers heard rumors of thieves' gold here, you'd be overrun. And they don't hesitate to kill to get what they want."

The Humans digested that information in shocked silence.

"That seems aggressive," Marlo said.

Gnedley pointed at the mushroom in Rachel's grasp. "*One* of those is worth more than the wealth of your world combined."

". . . I've been keeping them in plastic totes," she whispered.

"You can't keep them," Gnedley stressed. "We're far from

the reach of the Alliance. There's no aid nearby." He thought of how easily this situation could spiral, and shuddered. "It would become a free-for-all. I'm begging—"

"Wait," Marlo said. "Where did Lemon go?"

They all regarded the room, now absent of one Lemon Peabody.

"Did she take a mushroom?" Rachel demanded.

"Wow," Marlo said, her voice full of pride. Gnedley and Rachel turned in silent question. "Sorry. *Bad* Lemon . . . but also, I'm a little impressed at how stealthy that was?"

Unfortunately, Gnedley doubted she could be stealthy enough to stay out of harm's way.

CHAPTER 20

What was I thinking?

I rushed away from Marlo's, stolen mushroom in hand.

Truth was, I didn't think. Gnedley's words had sunk in and I found myself sneaking out, stealing a highly illegal fungi as I went.

What's the *plan*, Lemon? I escaped into my backyard, mind running a mile a minute.

Pirates. Smugglers. They had access to all kinds of stuff. More stuff than Gnemo?

Maybe I could bargain with them. Bargain with Gnilsson—

This was dumb. And dangerous. I took a step back toward Marlo's.

But it could work.

Last chance to help Grandpa?

I shook my head, gripping the mushroom—not too tight, I reminded myself. He wouldn't want to be helped this way.

"What are you doing?" I smacked my forehead with the mushroom-free hand.

"That's what I'd like to know."

I looked up to see Dad stepping off the deck into the yard— *Dad!*

A quick shuffle had the mushroom hidden behind my back.

"You're supposed to be grounded," he said. "But I come home to find you missing? I was worried si—"

"I can explain." I said, cutting in before he built up steam. "You're never going to believe this, but I hope you do. You pretty much have to."

He made a weird noise, like *hnnngh*, and stared at me with a constipated expression on his face. This was it. I'd finally pushed Patrick Peabody too far.

"Dad?" I took a step closer when he didn't move. Then I realized he wasn't moving at all. *"Dad?"* Reaching out to touch him, I gasped when my hand hit an invisible wall.

"Portable tractor-beam force field," said a voice behind him. I peered around to see Gnilsson with a small flashing cube in one hand. "Used to transport larger samples."

"Let him go."

Gnilsson tsked as he held the cube from my reach. "He's perfectly safe for now."

I gritted my teeth. "What do you want?"

"That belongs to me." He gestured at the mushroom in my hand.

Every fiber of my being recoiled at the thought of handing it over, but one look at Dad and I obeyed. It wasn't worth the risk.

"Come along," Gnilsson said, pocketing the mushroom. He lifted the cube, causing Dad to float over the grass. "Back to the ship."

"What if someone sees?" I motioned to all of the *broad daylight* surrounding us.

"Take my arm and the portable shield will cover you." He pointed to a triangle on his shirt. "The tractor beam has a cloaking function for your father."

Trying to stall seemed like asking for trouble. A quick look around showed no Gnedley, Marlo, or Rachel riding to the rescue. If they didn't realize . . .

Maybe I could leave a clue.

"Walk," Gnilsson snarled.

"Calm down!" I exclaimed. "I'm walking. Look at me go, left foot, right foot, left—"

"Walk silently."

"Yup," I whispered. "Tippy-toes."

No one batted an eyelash as we passed. Not one double take for the little green gnome steering the floating angry man down the sidewalk and into the woods. Quinn and the JFR group didn't miss a beat. All too soon, we were at the clearing.

Gnilsson strode through the barrier and dropped our cloaking.

Great. We were extra trapped now.

Captain Gnemo emerged from the ship, Gneelix and Gnog flanking her on either side. "Commander Gnilsson," she said. "You brought guests."

I waved weakly.

"Everyone into the hold," Gnilsson said as he brandished a metal stick.

"The laser pruner?" Gneelix scoffed. "Stop. You're embarrassing yourself."

There was a quick blaze of light and a harsh buzz. I blinked until I could see again. Gneelix stood stock-still, her orange hat faintly smoking where the tip had been cut off.

"Amazing how strong these can get with a little tinkering," Gnilsson said with a slow smirk. "Test me again. Please."

She curled her lip at him, but she followed the rest of the crew into the hold while we brought up the rear. I looked around in surprise. It was bigger than it appeared from outside. Crates and storage units lined the walls. Not many places to hide—worse yet, no easy exits in sight.

Aside from the one blocked by the armed gnome.

Gnilsson locked the crew in an empty unit and pushed me and Dad into another, directly across. He entered a code on the wall, and iridescent light rippled over the entrance to our makeshift cell. Another barrier shield. With a click on the cube, my dad crashed to the floor.

"Dad!" I bolted over to help him sit up as he groaned.

"Sit tight," Gnilsson said. "I've got a schedule to keep." Walking over to one of the crates, he lifted the lid, allowing a golden glow to seep out before he deposited the mushroom I'd given him inside.

"How did we miss . . . this whole time—" Gneelix raged. "*You* caused the crash. Cut the comms. *Damaged. My. Ship.* I'll make you pay, you odious piece of Xuirzix scum!"

"Language," Gnilsson tutted, typing rapidly on a device. "Relax. I'll be off your precious ship soon enough." He walked away, leaving the rest of us in silence.

"What's going on?" Dad croaked.

"Nothing good," I replied. Nothing good at all.

He peered over and frowned groggily. "Where are your *shoes*?"

Gnedley

Gnedley scooped up the remaining mushrooms in a sample bag, activated his shield, and dashed into the yard.

Lemon was nowhere in sight.

"Gnedley, don't leave," Marlo called as she and Rachel ran after him.

"I'm here," he assured her, and she jumped.

"So weird," she said, waving a hand to his left. "But good idea. We don't want people freaking out while we're looking for Lemon. Whatever she's up to."

"Hopefully she didn't get far with my mushroom," Rachel grumbled.

"Not your mushroom," Gnedley pointed out. Again.

"Focus," Marlo said, hands on her hips, deep in thought.

"Let's check her house first." She led them through the yard before stopping suddenly.

"What is it?" Gnedley asked.

"Lemon's shoe."

Gnedley scrutinized the battered blue footwear on the ground. "How can you be sure?"

"Trust me," Marlo said.

"Do you think something happened?" Rachel bit her lip.

"People don't normally walk off without a shoe," Marlo said. "Not even Lemon."

"Commander Gnilsson." The implications filled Gnedley with dread. "He must have followed the trackers and spotted Lemon with the mushroom."

"He took her?" Marlo's lips pressed into a thin line.

"I told you he was dangerous . . . ," Gnedley began.

"Not really an 'I told you so' moment, Gnedley," she snapped. "More of a 'how do we get my friend back in one piece' sort of deal."

Rachel gasped quietly. "Look." She pointed down the street. Another blue shoe sat in the middle of the sidewalk.

"This is the route we take to the park." Marlo said, running ahead to grab the shoe. "She's leaving a trail. They're going to the ship, right?"

Gnedley was certain that was exactly where they were

headed. It was an alarming move. If Gnilsson was no longer concerned with Captain Gnemo discovering his actions—

"I must return to the ship immediately," Gnedley said.

"If Lemon's in trouble, I'm coming too," Marlo said immediately.

"When I say dangerous," Gnedley wondered, "does that mean something different on your planet?"

"She's. My. Friend."

"I won't be able to keep you out of harm's way if you're seen."

"Hello, solution." Marlo held up the mushroom still cupped in her hand, a daring gleam in her eye.

Of all the—

"Absolutely not," Gnedley said, crossing his arms over his chest. "I forbid it."

"Earth's not part of your Alliance, so you can't forbid squat," Marlo said. "*And* if the situation was reversed, Lemon would do the same. For any of us."

Rachel grimaced. "'What would Lemon do?' is not the best way to evaluate our choices."

"This is not up for debate!" Gnedley exclaimed.

The Humans ignored him.

Marlo stepped over to Rachel. "I know things got weird with Lemon and this is a big ask," she said. "You don't have to come. You can keep your mushrooms—"

"No, she can't," Gnedley said, exasperated.

"I'll understand," Marlo continued. "Lemon too."

Was his translator malfunctioning?

He should lower his shield. Remind them of his presence.

"Don't you think this might be too much for us to handle?" Rachel asked.

Finally. The voice of reason.

"There's no time to get help." Marlo laughed mirthlessly. "Who'd believe us anyway?"

"We can't involve more Humans," Gnedley jumped in. "Your friend has no time to lose. I *must* return to the ship. Alone." He underscored the point, since it seemed hard for them to grasp.

"Okay," Rachel said, and Gnedley smiled until he realized she was addressing Marlo.

"Yeah?" Marlo's face lit up.

"Gnedley's right—our whole planet is at stake," Rachel explained. "We have to help."

"I am a capable member of the Alliance—"

"Besides." Rachel held up the mushroom *she'd* apparently also kept hold of. These Humans! "I can't pass up an opportunity to study this experience firsthand," she said.

Marlo grinned, laying the mushroom down on her palm. "For Lemon."

"And for science," Rachel added, doing the same.

The two Humans smashed their fists on their mushrooms, and before Gnedley could say impetuous, sparks flew and they were enveloped in a cloud of golden gas.

A choked cough drifted out.

"Yup," Marlo said faintly. "Definitely forgot about the smell."

CHAPTER 21

"Are you okay?" Dad pulled me over, eyes scanning me from head to toe.

"I'm fine," I said, straightening his glasses for him. "You were the one who got frozen or whatever that was."

He winced as he stumbled to his feet. Our cargo hold was tight for space, and Dad could barely stand without his head brushing the ceiling. He fumbled at the wall, getting his bearings.

"Where are we?"

"You're on the *Gnar Five*," Captain Gnemo said from across the bay. "My ship."

Dad spun around at the sound of her voice, and his breath caught. He slowly stepped forward, flinching when he ran into the barrier.

Gnemo stood calmly at the edge of their unit, Gneelix and Gnog on either side.

"Dad," I said, excited for this moment despite our circumstances. "This is *Gnemo*."

"No, she's not," he ground out.

Captain Gnemo shot me a confused frown, but I didn't know what to say.

"She can't be." He lifted a shaking finger to stab in her direction. "Because *Gnemo* isn't *real*. He made her up."

Captain Gnemo sucked in a breath. "You're Walter's son?"

"His name is Patrick," I said.

"Don't tell her that," Dad ordered. "She doesn't get to know anything about me."

"Dad, why—"

"Because she *ruined our lives*!" He slapped his hands against the barrier and it buzzed angrily until he pulled them back, tightened into fists at his side. Tears were running down his face. I'd seen him angry and upset before, but this . . .

He looked crushed.

"Whatever you did . . ." His voice broke. "Whatever you said to him? My dad was never the same." He took a trembling breath and I grabbed his hand, pulling him from the force field.

"Come on, Dad. Come here."

Breaking his stare with Gnemo, Dad let me lead him

farther into our cell. He collapsed onto a crate, burying his face in his hands. I didn't know if I should hug him or leave him be. I didn't want to make things worse. I'd never seen him so . . . cracked open.

"Dad?" I whispered.

"Not now, Lemon," he muttered, and I backed off.

"What's all this shouting?" Gnilsson strode up the ramp. "Some of us are trying to conduct business."

"Go away," Gneelix snapped. "No one wants to listen to you."

"Hmm, well, tell me something I don't know." Gnilsson perched on a box in front of the gnomes.

"You think your cap looks stylish when you wear it at that angle, but it really looks like you don't know how hats work," Gneelix said flatly.

"Do shut up, Gneelix." He snatched off his cap and stuffed it in his pocket. "Have a little more respect for the gnome holding your future in his hands."

Dad looked up at that, and I held a finger to my lips. Better to stay out of this.

"How can I respect someone whose family had to *buy* him a spot on a ship?" she sneered. "Even then, the *Gnar Five* was the only one who would take you."

"Enough!" Gnemo shouted as they snarled at each other.

She nudged Gneelix back from the barrier. "Gnilsson—"

"Going to offer me one of those famous second chances, Captain?" he asked softly.

"This *was* your second chance." Regret deepened every line of her face. "You could have been a great officer, sprout."

His shoulders tightened at that. "I guess we'll never know."

A beep sounded and he prowled off deeper into the ship. The gnomes huddled up, talking quietly, and I moved over to the wall beside Dad, sliding down to take a seat.

"That guy seems nice," he said mildly, surprising a laugh out of me.

"Don't judge the rest of them by him," I said, jerking my chin at the crew. "They're actually pretty cool."

Dad hummed as he shuffled off his crate and I scooted over to tuck into his side.

"You okay?"

"Not really." He wrapped an arm around my shoulders, tugging me in close. "You?"

"It's not how I planned the big alien reveal," I said. "There would've been a party."

"Cake?" Dad asked, sliding me a sideways look.

"Obviously." Would've been green on the inside too. I kicked at our cramped cage. "At least now you know Grandpa was telling the truth and you can make up."

"Lemon." He gripped his knees and pressed his forehead against them. Looking up after a beat, he blew out a heavy sigh. "It's not that easy, okay?"

"I kinda think it is."

"You know, I experienced Grandpa's story in real time," he said. "Day by day. Researching space and making charts. Trying to guess when his alien would return."

That sounded familiar.

He shook his head. "I believed him completely." Dad caught the look on my face, and his lips twisted wryly. "I did," he said. "Even when the jokes started. Walt wasn't bothered, so I tried not to be. But the jokes kept coming and the alien never did."

"That's when you stopped."

"Eventually it was too hard," he said. "It started to make me mad. Still does."

"You know Gnemo is real now," I said. "Doesn't that help? Can't you—"

"Get over it?" Dad thunked his head against the wall. He stayed quiet, thinking.

"I came downstairs one night," he finally said. "Late. For water or something. And Walter was on the porch, looking at the stars. He did that, I found out. Stared at the sky. Every night. We could have the *best* day, and he'd still end up on the porch."

Dad hesitated, scratching at his cheek.

"I think *that*, more than anything, is what I couldn't take," he said. "Feeling like he was always missing something. I know he loved me. Loved my mom. But I hated seeing him out there and feeling like we weren't enough."

He looked over and met my eyes. "Part of the reason I didn't want you searching for aliens with him was because I worried you'd end up feeling that way too."

Oh. *Oh.* "I always thought you were upset *because* I believed in Grandpa's aliens," I admitted. "That you were disappointed in me."

"Lemon, no." Dad hugged me. "Frustrated maybe, but never disappointed." He squeezed me tighter. "I'm sorry. I really haven't handled any of this very well."

I sniffled into his shirt. "Are you going to talk to Grandpa?"

He didn't say anything, and I sat back.

"It's more complicated now that he's sick," Dad said.

"I thought once you knew Gnemo was real—"

"Me and your grandpa . . ." He gave me another squeeze. "It's not your responsibility to fix," he said. "That's up to us."

"But you want to try?"

"Yeah," Dad said. "I do." He slapped a hand against his knee. "But first we've got to figure out how to get you off this ship."

"Both of us, you mean."

"Do you know how to disable that barrier?" He gestured around our tiny room. "See anywhere big enough for me to fit through?"

"But—"

"Our best bet is to find a vent or something you can squeeze out of." Dad's eyes scanned the walls, but our makeshift prison was seamlessly put together. "Or create a distraction," he said. "Do something to make that guy open the door so you can get away."

I scowled at him. "I'm not gonna *leave* you here."

"To find *help*," he said. "It's the only way."

"Not the only way," I said quietly, and nodded across the hold. "The gnomes could help."

Dad instantly shied away from that. "I don't—"

"They're the professionals," I said. "We should work together."

He looked over at the gnomes and rolled his eyes. "The professionals are eating marshmallows."

I climbed up on my knees to peek.

Doctor Gnog was rummaging in a bag I recognized, while Gneelix held another one open to Gnemo. "Try one," she said. "They're not terrible."

Captain Gnemo accepted a marshmallow, taking a small

bite. "Quite delicious," she said with a delighted noise. "Thank you, Gneelix."

Dad lurched to his feet. "Are you going to sit there eating junk?" he whisper-shouted at them. "Or are you going to get us out of here?"

Doctor Gnog clutched the bag tighter, looking mortally offended.

"Can't your badges break through, like the barrier outside?" I asked, grasping at ideas.

Gneelix paused, marshmallow halfway to her mouth. "You think we'd be sitting here if we could?"

"Gnilsson altered the code when he locked us in," Gnog explained.

"Oh." I sagged against the wall, stumped.

"All is not lost." Gnemo waved a marshmallow in the air. "Don't forget—we have a gnome on the outside."

Gnedley

Gnedley had no idea what he was doing.

The Captain had said one wrong move could change the course of an entire planet.

Was attempting to rescue the crew and take back the *Gnar Five* with nothing but two invisible Humans at his side the correct move?

It was doubtful, but it was the only move Gnedley had.

"Marlo," he whispered as they approached the clearing. "Rachel? Location status."

"We're here," said Marlo's voice beside his ear.

He *did not* jump.

"What do you want us to do?" Rachel's voice asked.

"Stay quiet," Gnedley said. "And hold on to me while we

infiltrate the shield." He flinched as one arm hit him in the face and another on the ear.

"Sorry," Marlo said. "We really didn't think this 'everyone's invisible' thing through."

He grabbed the hands and set them on his shoulders, then activated his key.

"Keep close," Gnedley murmured once they were on the other side. He watched with a sinking feeling as Gnilsson marched around the ship, typing into his communicator. The absence of the others spelled a leap forward in the commander's plan. They had to hurry.

"We need to sneak up the ramp onto the ship."

"And then what?" Rachel whispered.

"We find Captain Gnemo." She would know how to proceed. "On my signal." He waited until Gnilsson headed toward the other end of the clearing. "Go."

He scuttled across the grass to the ship. A quick search of the hold revealed his captive crewmates, along with Lemon and another Human.

"Captain." Gnedley said, flicking off his shield.

"Gnedley!" Lemon called quietly from her side of the hold. "You made it! This is my dad, Patrick. Say hi to Gnedley, Dad."

"He's not the only one," Marlo said. "Lemon, you nugget! What were you thinking?"

Lemon looked eagerly around the room. "Marlo? Are you mad? You're totally mad. I can't see your face, but I can *feel* your energy." Her eyes widened. "I can't see your face! *Did you smash a mushroom?*"

"It smelled *so bad*," Marlo said.

"Much more intense from inside the cloud," Rachel added.

"Rachel!" Lemon cheered.

"Mushrooms?" Patrick's face filled with alarm. "Bad guy's mushrooms? What—did you *eat* them? How are you invisible? What am I going to tell your parents?"

"I can't believe you smashed the stink bombs of doom for me," Lemon cooed.

"Not just for you," Rachel said. "For the planet. And science."

"Still touched!" Lemon pressed against the barrier, ignoring the buzz. "Get me out of here so I can hug your invisible face!"

Gnedley approached the keypad on the unit holding his crewmates. "Any guess as to what the code could be?"

"Statistically," Rachel's voice popped up beside him, and Gnedley *did not* jump. "Most people use a significant date."

The hold was silent while everyone racked their brains.

"His birthday," Marlo suggested.

Gnedley looked at the crew and Gneelix shrugged.

"You don't know his birthday," Lemon exclaimed, shaking her head. "I think we're uncovering the root of his many grievances."

"I know it," Doctor Gnog said, and proceeded to rattle off a series of numbers. Everyone stared at the doctor, who shrugged. "I'm the doctor. I read his file."

Fingers flying, Gnedley typed it in. And cringed when the panel flashed red.

"If the second attempt is wrong, the alarm sounds," Gneelix warned.

"Put in today's date," Captain Gnemo said.

"Captain?" Gnedley tilted his head in question.

"Trust me, Ensign."

Gnedley typed in the date, and the force field on the crew's unit went off with a blip. He slumped in a moment of relief echoed by everyone in the hold. "How did you guess?"

"A significant date, as Rachel Morris surmised," she said. "Today is the day Gnilsson becomes the richest gnome in the universe."

"Ugh." Lemon snorted. "He's the worst."

Gnedley made quick work of releasing her and her father and passed Lemon her shoes. Two invisible forces immediately knocked into her, laughing as she tried to grab hold.

"Everyone down here, please." Captain Gnemo motioned

to a corner out of sight from the ramp. Patrick Peabody looked pained when Lemon yanked him over to join them.

The clock was ticking. Pirates were on their way.

They needed a plan full of right moves.

"What's our next step, Captain?" Gnedley asked, and Gnemo smiled grimly.

"We take back our ship."

CHAPTER 22

"Maybe I should use a mushroom too," I whispered to my invisible friends as we crept through the hold.

"Don't even think—" A rumbling noise cut off Dad's protest. "What is that?"

"Another ship," Gnemo said grimly. "Gnilsson's disabled the barrier to let them in."

She ducked behind a pile of crates close to the ramp, and we followed just in time. The clearing in front of the ship was suddenly filled by a sleek black vessel.

"Why is it so shiny?" I whispered, taking in the many fins. "Looks fancy."

"Piracy pays well," Doctor Gnog said.

"Bells and whistles," Gneelix grunted. "The *Gnar Five*

could outrun that flash any day."

Rachel made a doubtful noise beside me.

"Is there not a back door we could be escaping out of?" Dad asked.

Captain Gnemo shushed us, leaning forward to watch. The stairs were descending from the new ship, and a set of boots emerged. I was about to see my first space pirate.

I was not disappointed.

The owner of the boots was *massive*. Their muscular upper half strained against a grimy, worn jacket, and their legs looked like tree trunks. Huge, pointy-tipped horns grew out of the top of their head, spanning the width of the doorway, and their face ended in a flat snout.

"Is . . . is that," Marlo breathed. "A *minotaur*?"

"Captain Minoz," Gnedley whispered, shaking from head to toe. "They say anyone who crosses him gets—" He jolted as the pirate snorted a flame out of one nostril and launched a gob of fiery spit that smoldered on the ground.

"Volcanic phlegm." Rachel's voice floated with reverence.

"So space pirates are a bit terrifying," Marlo whispered, and I had to agree.

A few crew members filed out behind Captain Minoz. One seemed to be a small and angry scaly creature, the next . . . mostly rocks. The last had shiny skin and purple wings spanning their spindly seven-foot-tall form. Captain Minoz let out a series of bone-shaking growls as Gnilsson approached, and I poked Gnedley in frustration.

"What are they saying?" I hissed.

"One moment." Gneelix rummaged around in a crate, retrieving what looked like little curved antennas with a soft ball on the end. "Backup portable translators." She demonstrated sticking the soft end in our ears and held them out for us to grab.

Translator firmly in place, I could eavesdrop.

"Where's my shipment?" Captain Minoz growled.

"Where's my payment?" Gnilsson replied, crossing his arms with a smirk.

I would *not* be antagonizing the colossal pirate minotaur if I was him.

Minoz towered over Gnilsson. "I didn't travel to the middle of nowhere to be insulted. Find myself wondering if ten thieves' shrooms was worth the trip."

Gnilsson made a show of considering the captain's words. "I might be convinced to part with fifteen . . . with a little incentive."

A roar shook the clearing.

"Twenty?" he squeaked.

"This your ship?" Minoz pointed at the *Gnar Five* and we

all ducked. "Think I'll take it too," he mused. "Could get a nice price for the scrap."

Captain Gnemo pulled Gneelix down as she tried to lunge forward. "Settle," Gnemo said, quietly. "We'll make our move soon enough."

Minoz spat another glob of fire phlegm at Gnilsson's feet. He danced back with a yelp, stubbing his smoking boot out in the grass.

"Are you planning to make that move before or after he catches fire?" Dad asked.

"I suppose I should step in." Gnemo stood and straightened her uniform. "Stay here. I'll deal with this."

"Um," Marlo said as Gnemo walked away. "Should she be going alone?"

"Without a fire extinguisher?" Rachel added.

"Gnemo is more than capable." Doctor Gnog waved off our concerns, though Gnedley looked less convinced. He leaped up from our huddle, snatching something out of the closest crate, and charged ahead of Gnemo. She stumbled in surprise.

"Gnedley . . ." She reached out, but he was already facing off with Gnilsson and the pirates, wielding a ceramic garden gnome.

"Isn't that Mrs. Harrison's?" Dad asked with a squint.

Captain Minoz's mouth dropped open in a mighty bellow.

In one fell swoop, Gnedley was scooped up, tiny body squeezed in a giant hand. The statue dropped to the grass.

"Gnedley!" I cried. Scrambling out from our hiding spot, I ran down the ramp.

"Lemon!" Dad shouted, thumping after me.

I couldn't sit by and let Gnedley get squished. My heart pounded, blood thundering in my ears. Think, Lemon, think! Distract the angry pirate so Gnedley can get away! How?

There.

I pounced and spun around, swinging Mrs. Harrison's garden gnome through the air.

Gnedley

This was how he died.

Squished to death by a pirate captain.

Gnedley wondered if there was a section for that on the incident report.

His only thought as he'd watched Gnemo leave the ship was that none of this would be happening if he had gone to her at the start. Gnedley couldn't let her step into harm's way over his own mistake. He'd grabbed the first thing he could lay hands on and he'd run out, but even that proved to be a futile move once Lemon chased after him, followed by her father.

Foolishly brave Humans.

Gnedley groaned. Captain Minoz's hand was like a vise.

A hairy, malodorous vise. He squirmed, and hot breath blew across his face as Minoz snorted.

"Let the Humans go," Gnedley rasped, earning himself another bellow directly in his ear.

"Lemon, stop!" Gnemo shouted.

He caught a glimpse of her rushing over to grab the gnome statue out of the Human's hands. At this rate, the cursed statue might be the only one left standing.

Lemon's father guided her away as Captain Gnemo stepped up to Gnedley and his captor. "Captain Minoz," she said. "Would you be so kind as to release my ensign?"

Gnedley waited for her to be obliterated in a ball of fiery spittle. He shook in Minoz's grasp—*was* he shaking? Or was that—

Captain Minoz was *laughing*. *"GNEMO!"*

Wait.

What?

CHAPTER 23

The pirate captain erupted in *giggles*.

Dad tried to put me behind him, but I held my ground. No way was I missing this.

"What are you doing here?" Captain Minoz carefully set Gnedley down and clasped a hand on Gnemo's shoulder. More like her entire shoulder and upper arm. It was a big hand.

She patted his fingers. "This is my ship, Min."

Min?

Minoz whipped around, an incredulous expression on his face. "You were going to give me *Gnemo's* ship?"

"I was not . . . I—" Gnilsson didn't have a chance to finish that thought as Minoz swiftly tossed him across the clearing, knocking the wind out of him.

"My apologies," Minoz said. "The deal was set up in good faith."

Gnemo scrunched her nose. "You thought a deal to obtain highly illegal fungi was legitimate?"

"Smuggler legitimate." He waved a hand. "There's a scale."

"With a deep, deep slide." Gnemo laughed.

"Now . . ." Minoz pulled her out of earshot of his crew, but close enough for us to hear. "This puts me in a tight spot," he murmured. "You don't become captain of a pirate ship by being soft. I can't let this go."

"I've got you covered." Gnemo nodded and stepped back. "Captain Minoz," she called, catching the attention of his crew. "Relinquishing this deal would be a great service for which you deserve recompense." She steepled her fingers under her chin. "It's time."

Everyone hung on her next words.

"I'm hereby clearing . . . the Debt," Captain Gnemo said gravely.

I choked out a laugh as the pirate crew jabbered at each other, recognizing the seriousness of this offer. Galaxies apart, the currency of friendship remained the same.

"The Debt." Captain Minoz blinked. "The one you've held on to since our academy days and you're willing to consider it paid? *In full?*"

"Absolutely." Captain Gnemo nodded.

Captain Minoz sighed deeply, singeing the surrounding grass. "Done," he said, waggling a finger at her. "But it'll be a different story next time, Gnemo."

"Join the Alliance and there won't be a next time!" she hollered.

"Nice seeing you," he said over his shoulder with a roguish grin as he and his crew entered their ship.

She chuckled and smiled back.

The stairs rose behind them and the cloaking shields activated, disappearing the ship from view. With a rumble and a faint *whoosh*, the pirates departed, and all was quiet.

"Get back!"

We whipped around to see Gnilsson standing in the loading bay, laser pruner in hand, forcing Gnog and Gneelix down the ramp. Thank goodness Marlo and Rachel were still invisible. Hopefully they'd already sneaked away.

"You may have ruined this deal," Gnilsson said. "But I've still got the mushrooms and I'm taking the ship."

"Oh, for the—" Gnemo grabbed the gnome statue at her feet and lobbed it at Gnilsson. It sailed through the air to bounce off his forehead, and his eyes rolled back as he crumpled to the floor of the loading dock. "That's quite enough out of you."

He definitely deserved that, but also . . . "Is he okay?"

"Nothing a nap won't fix," Gnemo said. She turned to face the rest of the crew. "Gnedley, assist Doctor Gnog with securing Gnilsson in the hold. Gneelix, reactivate the barrier shield." She surveyed the ship. "We should be up and running quickly."

"Aye, Captain." The crew hopped into action while a glimmer caught the corner of my eye. Marlo and Rachel slowly started to reappear.

"You're back!" I grabbed them both for an epic group hug.

"The rest of our heroic Humans," Gnemo said. "Thank you for your assistance."

I flailed a little bit. "Are we not gonna get the backstory?"

"Hmm?" Gnemo's faked-innocence face wasn't fooling me.

"With 'GNEMO!' and 'Min!' and the *Debt* and—" I flapped my hands through the air. "All of what just happened?"

"Min would adore your impression of him," she said dryly.

I stood, hands on hips, waiting.

"Minoz and I were at the academy together," Gnemo said. "Though I joined the Alliance after, and he . . . did not. We got into our fair share of trouble during that time. One day he needed my help, and I gave it."

"Help with what?" Marlo asked.

"That"—Gnemo winked—"is between me and Min."

She laughed when we groaned, and Dad shuffled awkwardly at the side of our little group. "If we're in the clear," he said. "I should get the girls home."

It felt too soon to say goodbye.

"A moment, please." Gnemo led Dad and me to the side of the ship, leaving Marlo to hold Rachel back as she poked at the remains of Minoz's still-smoldering snot.

"I must apologize," Gnemo said, looking up at Dad.

"For what specifically?" Dad asked warily. "Because I can think of a few things, some just from today."

"Be nice!" I whispered, pulling on his sleeve.

"It's quite all right," Gnemo said. "Your father has a point. And I do apologize for today's events. Your family should never have been pulled into Gnilsson's misdeeds."

"I pulled myself into some of this," I admitted. "Plus, Gnilsson should take responsibility for his own mess! If—"

"Lemon," my dad interrupted, half exasperated, half amused. "Let her finish."

Gnemo nodded her thanks, taking a moment before continuing. "I've come to realize," she said, "that I never properly considered what effect my visit with Walter would have on his life."

Dad huffed and I nudged him, a reminder to hear Gnemo out.

"Given that I wasn't able to return," Gnemo said. "I think I never *wanted* to consider it."

"But you're here now!" I pointed out.

"A new chance," Gnemo agreed. "I'm sorry, Patrick. I hope to leave this time with better understanding on both sides."

"I always wondered what I'd say if I ever got to meet you." Dad said, searching for some kind of answer in Gnemo's face. "Why Walter?"

"In all honesty," she said. "I came across him by accident."

"I know, but why stay?" Dad pressed her. "Why let him know about aliens when you could've left him in the dark?"

"He started talking." Captain Gnemo shrugged helplessly. "I couldn't walk away."

That I understood. Grandpa Walt could talk with anybody about anything.

"I'd never met someone unaware of life on other planets," she said. "It was fascinating to hear what he thought. He was so curious. I couldn't answer his questions fast enough."

Dad and I laughed a bit at that. Classic Walter.

"He was like a new recruit," she said. "Eager to soak it all in. It was infectious." Gnemo smiled fondly at the memory. "Walter put a face to the mission that night, and I'm a better captain for it."

She reached out to grasp Dad's hand. "It was *my honor* to meet him."

Dad nodded shakily as he swiped at his eyes.

"Captain Gnemo?" I swallowed against the lump in my throat.

Fate had given me a second chance, and I couldn't pass it up.

"I grew up with Grandpa's stories of how amazing you were," I said. "Then we finally met and I realized—you're even more amazing than I dreamed." I tucked shaking hands into my pockets. "Feels like there's no limit to what's possible in your world."

"There *are* limits," Gnemo said gently.

"You're still way beyond us," I said, gathering my breath to get it all out there. "Could you help Grandpa Walt? Since you're here? And he's your friend?"

"Lemon . . . ," Dad said.

The captain looked confused. "Help him how?"

"His illness I told you about? It's something in his brain that affects his memory." If you don't ask, you'll never know, I reminded myself. "Could you cure him?"

"*Oh.*" Dad crouched to pull me in for a hug. "Oh, sweetie."

He didn't say anything for a while. I pushed away to peek at his face.

"Is this why you've been working so hard to find them?" he asked in a hoarse whisper.

"I always wanted to find them," I said. "For Grandpa. And.

for you." I leaned against his shoulder. "But once I saw what they could do . . . I had to try. For all of us."

"I love you." He squeezed me again. "And I love that you wanted to help your grandpa, but . . ." Dad looked to Captain Gnemo, and my heart sank. Her face told me everything I needed to know.

"I wish I could, but at this moment, a cure is beyond our reach." She shook her head and sighed. "Brains are complicated entities. On every planet."

Part of me knew that would be the answer, but I never would've forgiven myself if I hadn't asked. "Thank you, Captain," I said, sniffling. "I can't wait to tell Grandpa I met you. And that Dad did too." I pictured it. "Not sure he'll believe that part."

Dad chuckled quietly.

"I may not be able to offer medical assistance," Captain Gnemo said as she accepted my hug. "But I believe I can grant your other request."

Gnedley

Gnedley tumbled Gnilsson into a storage unit while Doctor Gnog keyed in a new code. The commander groaned and rolled over, but stayed silent after that.

"He'll be fine," the doctor said after a quick scan. They steered Gnedley toward the end of the hold to sit on a crate and checked him for injuries after his encounter with Minoz.

"Minor bruising, Ensign," they declared. "But no worse for wear."

Gnedley's ribs begged to differ.

Pulling a bag of marshmallows from nowhere, Gnog offered it to Gnedley after snagging their own treat. "Quite the day," they said, chewing thoughtfully.

Gnedley took one and stared out at the Humans, talking

and smiling in the clearing. Quite the day indeed. He was going to miss this strange little planet and its occupants. "Doctor, how long have you been on the IC route?"

"Longer than you've been alive, sprout."

"How—how do you handle it?" he asked. "Always having to stay separate like we do?"

"Hmm." Gnog nodded. "The isolation can be hard. Especially after an experience like you've had," they said. "You must remember that eventually an IC planet *will* be ready to step out and join the universe. It's a truly wondrous thing to witness."

Doctor Gnog stared into the distance, lost in wistful remembrance. "It may not happen for 525-1 in your lifetime," they continued. "Certainly not in mine. But isn't it our duty to prepare the crews that come after us to welcome them?"

"I hadn't thought about it like that," Gnedley admitted.

"Everything you do on this voyage matters, sprout," Gnog said. "Even if you never live to see where the ripples from your actions end."

"Gnedley! Gnog!" Captain Gnemo called. "Come out here, please."

"We have a mission to complete before launch," she said once the crew was together. "Doctor Gnog and Chief Gneelix will remain to keep an eye on Gnilsson. Gnedley, with me."

Before Gnedley could ask what the mission *was*, Captain Gnemo had the Humans ready at the barrier. She and Gnedley passed them all through and then activated their shields.

Lemon's father startled. "Where'd they go?"

"It's okay, Dad," Lemon said. "They have a special cloaking thing, but they're still here."

He searched the air. "That's gonna take getting used to. They're okay to follow us?"

"We can see *you*," Captain Gnemo replied, amusement coloring her tone.

"Right." Patrick blushed. He headed into the woods, and the rest of them trailed behind.

The forest was quiet. Gnedley appreciated the moment of peace. He was not the same gnome who had first stepped onto the *Gnar Five*, and for that he was grateful. He'd never trade in what he'd learned the last few days . . . but he would take a nap.

The Humans led them out of the park and down sidewalk after sidewalk until they halted in front of a large brick building. Patrick Peabody entered and spoke to another Human at the desk before motioning for the rest of them to file in.

Gnedley looked around freely under the cover of his shield. The building hummed with peaceful activity. Most rooms had elderly Humans asleep in beds or reading in chairs. More than one had an entertainment unit on. He stopped short as the group paused in front of a doorway. Captain Gnemo entered, stepping to the side before lowering her shield. Gnedley did the same. The Humans moved in after, and Marlo shut the door behind them.

A Human slept in a worn brown recliner at the center of the room. His lined face, craggy with age, was relaxed, mouth open in a gentle snore.

"Grandpa," Lemon said, stepping forward to wake him.

Oh.

The importance of their expedition hit Gnedley in a flash.

A gift from Gnemo before a final farewell.

CHAPTER 24

My hand shook as I tapped Grandpa Walt's shoulder. Our last visit hadn't gone well, and part of me was steeled for a repeat.

But this time—

Dad was here.

And Gnemo.

Finally. *Gnemo.*

It still hurt that things weren't working out the way I *really* wanted them to, but at least I could give Grandpa *this.*

He woke from his snooze with a snort. "Wha—? What's going on?" He fumbled around, reaching until his fingers hit his glasses on the small side table. He rubbed them against his shirt before sliding them on.

"Hi, Grandpa," I said, hovering so he could see me clearly. "Sorry to wake you."

"Not to worry." He yawned. "Did I know you were coming by?"

"Nope. Surprise visit!"

He grinned back, holding my hand. "You know, you look more like your grandmother every day."

"Thanks, Grandpa." I swallowed hard.

Ugh. This was ridiculous. I was *excited*. We'd waited for so long and now Gnemo was here and I could barely speak. Tears swimming in my eyes, I looked to my dad for help.

He came to stand beside me. "Hi, Dad."

"Patrick," Grandpa Walt whispered. "What are you doing here?"

"Like Lemon said, surprise visit." Dad crouched by the chair. "We brought someone to see you."

Grandpa looked up as Gnemo stepped forward and reached to take his other hand. "Hello, Walter," she said, voice warm.

Confusion flitted across Grandpa's face.

Oh no.

My heart skipped a beat and I held my breath. The room went still as everyone else did the same.

Slowly Grandpa Walt's eyes widened, and he *beamed*.

"Gnemo," he said. "My old friend."

Epilogue

Two weeks had gone by since our alien adventure.

The gnomes had taken the last of the mushroom crop and confiscated everything Rachel had gathered, down to the last spore.

It was an ordeal.

We loaded them up with about twenty bags of marshmallows, which would hopefully last a couple of days at least.

And then they left. Disappearing in a blip as we waved.

Things in Linleydale were slowly getting back to normal. For the most part.

Rachel was appeased over the loss of her mushrooms by a very sneaky gift from Chief Gneelix, of all gnomes. A cluster of mushrooms allegedly close enough to a strand of Earth mushrooms to pass as a mutation. They were supposed to be extra good at the environmental decomposition thing? Rachel gave us a whole explanation with detailed charts.

Bottom line, she was in mycological heaven.

Our science sleepovers were now a regular event, and Marlo was helping her draft her Nobel Prize speech. Just in case.

Marlo was hard at work on her new novel. A space opera following a group of hapless explorers caught up in the shenanigans of a bootlegger. The start of a six-part series! She'd read a few chapters to us, and so far it was out of this world.

Heh.

Disappointingly, she continued to refuse to let me name a character. "Lemonia is never going to happen," she snapped during my last pitch. "Or Peabodicus. Stop."

I wasn't concerned. Plenty more ideas where those came from.

And me?

I was enjoying what was left of summer. Amazing how much free time I had now that Project Validation was done. I spent my days making sure Marlo and Rachel came up for air and visiting with Grandpa Walt.

The best thing was . . . I wasn't the only one filling up the visiting schedule.

"Time to go!" my dad called up the stairs.

"Coming," I hollered. Slipping my necklace on, I smiled at the green leaf attached to the chain before tucking it into my shirt and hustling to the front door.

"Have fun," Mom said, giving us each a kiss goodbye.

A few minutes later, we were sailing past the front desk of the retirement home and Nurse Edie waved at me. *Waved!* If that wasn't a sign of how much things had changed, I didn't know what was.

Loud snores rattled the door of Grandpa's room while we stood on the other side.

"Hrngargknngh."

Dad quirked an eyebrow and I stifled a laugh. He turned the handle, letting us into the room. I tiptoed to the chair where Grandpa was fast asleep. His glasses were nearly falling off his nose, and a book lay across his lap.

"Grandpa," I whispered.

The snoring increased.

Undeterred, I poked his shoulder. "Grandpa!"

He startled awake, slowly focusing until he peered at me owlishly. "Hello, dear! Did I know you were coming for a visit?"

"Yes," I laughed.

"Well, then." He rubbed his hands together. "Ready to work on our project?"

Our project . . . "Do you mean Project Validation? We finished that, remember?"

Grandpa caught sight of Dad and noticed the look we shared. He nodded, tapping the side of his nose with a wink.

Ah.

Today was not a great day.

"It's okay," I said. "Dad knows everything now."

Dad squatted beside the chair, his face only a little pinched. Coming here was still hard, but he was trying. "It's true," he said. "Even heard a few extra details from Gnemo herself."

"Gnemo?" Grandpa whispered. "You met her?"

There it was. Dad tugged me over by the hand and caught me in a side hug.

Grandpa forgetting things—important things—was hard. It was only going to get worse, and I was working on accepting that. Mom said I could have all the time I needed as long as we kept talking about it. That helped.

The other thing that helped, surprisingly enough, was having Dad here with me.

"He did," I said, clearing my throat. "Me too! Can you believe that? We had a whole adventure on their ship. And we brought Gnemo here to see you."

Grandpa blinked and I could almost see the memory come back to him.

"Oh my goodness," he said, pressing a hand against his mouth. He let out a shaky breath. "Yes. Gnemo was *here*. How . . . how could I forget that?" Grandpa knotted his fingers together in his lap and sighed. He looked up at us, mouth set.

"Tell me again," he said. "The whole story."

"The whole story, he says." Dad pulled over the footstool and took a seat. "I guess it started when Lemon ran off and I found her in the yard—"

"Noooo, Dad," I said, leaning on his shoulder. "Start at the beginning."

"The *beginning* beginning?"

"It's the way we do things around here." I grinned at him.

"Okay," he said, scooching over to make room for me. Grandpa settled into his chair, glasses back in place, ready to listen.

"It was a hot summer night," Dad began. "Hotter than it had any right to be, but that's the weather for you." He nudged me, and I jumped in.

"Turns out, it wasn't the least predictable thing to happen that night. . . ."

Acknowledgments

Much like Lemon and Project Validation, I've had a number of amazing people help me with Operation Garden Gnomes from Outer Space.

First of all, I would like to thank my editor, Martha Mihalick, for believing in this cast of slightly odd characters and giving them a safe place to land. And a huge thank-you to the rest of the Greenwillow and HarperCollins teams, including Virginia Duncan, Arianna Robinson, Tim Smith, Sylvie Le Floc'h, Emma Meyer, Lauren Levite, and the tireless folks of the marketing, publicity, and sales departments.

To my agent, Molly Ker Hawn, thank you for always being along for the ride with any idea I come up with. Your support and guidance mean the world to me.

Thank you to Andy Smith for the stellar cover art!

To my critique partners and friends, Laura Shovan, Timanda Wertz, Margaret Dilloway, Janet Johnson, and Rebecca Donnelly: thank you for your always helpful insight and endless encouragement.

Thank you to Jed A. Levine of CaringKind for the thoughtful notes and kind words.

To Jean Moir and the team at the Middlesex County Library: thank you for always supporting and cheering me on!

Thank you to my friends and family who always understand when I disappear into the writing cave. I love you all!

And the biggest thank-you forever to my mom and dad who believed in me and my dreams from day one. Love you to the moon and back!

CASEY LYALL is the author of the acclaimed picture book *A Spoonful of Frogs*, illustrated by Vera Brosgol, and Howard Wallace, P.I., a middle grade series. When she's not writing, she likes to bake, doodle, and learn extremely groan-worthy jokes to tell her friends. Casey Lyall lives in southwestern Ontario, where she also works at her local library. And yes, she absolutely believes in aliens.

www.caseylyall.com